An Audacious Partnership

CORINNE CAVANAUGH

E-Book ISBN: 979-8-9899591-2-9
Paperback ISBN: 979-8-9899591-4-3
Library of Congress Control Number: 2024919413

DEDICATION

For women who are brave enough to lead, and vulnerable enough to succeed in a partnership. In business and in life, you can stand for something together and still have fun along the way.

CONTENTS

ACKNOWLEDGMENTS

This book was inspired by several audacious partnerships I've been lucky to have in business and in life.

Thank you, R, for creating a safe space for us to become allies, protectors of each other, and fearless businesswomen. Thank you, Virginia, for being my silent partner over the years, and for cheering me on in all things business and Rotary.

Thank you to my mother-in-law, Rachel, for showing up in a big way so that I can live my dreams and support our family.

Finally, I want to thank my partner in life, Kyle, for demonstrating daily what gender equity looks like, and giving me the time and space to do audacious shit.

CONTENT WARNING

An Audacious Partnership highlights the differences between men and women in different age groups and circumstances through fictional events. Events encourage readers to think critically about complex relationship dynamics, both professional and personal, and ultimately how we can lift each other up.

There are scenes that are sexually charged and allude to sex occurring. Adult language.

1 FUCK YES OR NO

July 2019

"Have you heard of this motto, 'Fuck Yes or No'?" Brooke asked Kathy while reclining in a cream lounge chair adjacent to an immaculately kept outdoor pool.

She stared off into the distance, grateful for the temporary reprieve from her fast-paced life. A New Yorker for nearly a decade now, Brooke was used to the energy that zipped through the city air, and had leveraged that energy to become part-owner of the Beaufort Estate and accompanying endowment fund—the other half belonged to Kathy.

Taking a deep breath, Brooke considered how far she had come while in the city: from a fashion school dropout to online rental property super-host, and now an entrepreneur—a woman making her dreams a reality.

As she savored the views of the Hudson River that sprawled in the distance beyond her pink toenails, Brooke felt a deep gratitude for Eleanor and the lessons she had imparted during and after the contest. Converting the estate into a hotel and restaurant had not been easy, but when she spun out, Eleanor was always there—a phone call or email away—encouraging her to trust her ideas, buck convention, and go for it.

Considering Brooke's question, Kathy replied, "I don't think I've heard that before. Sounds a bit vulgar to me," she said, taking a sip of her coconut water in a lounger beside Brooke.

While Kathy had grown accustomed to the opulent life she and Brooke now had together, she could never quite shake the feeling that something could go wrong at any moment. She often lay awake at night, worried about something she couldn't quite put her finger on, getting a terrible night's sleep then, inevitably, drinking too many cups of coffee in the morning.

"Ha! I guess it does sound vulgar, but it's not really. 'Fuck Yes or No' was originally intended to help people decide if they wanted to continue dating someone, but I think of it more as an ideology—a philosophy to make any decision. Either something gives me 'fuck yes' vibes, or I don't do it."

Brooke had recently begun following this mantra for everything, from what to wear to which restaurant staff to hire—everything, that is, except dating. Her love life was nonexistent, one of the many things she had in common with Kathy. Brooke was fifteen years younger than her partner and had never married, while Kathy was single by way of divorce. They both envied Eleanor's breezy romantic relationship with Oliver. The couple, who were now gallivanting all over the world, were fully committed to each other and madly in love—uninhibited by the institution of marriage.

"When you put it that way, I guess it's a clever tool to get down to brass tacks, although I don't think I'll utter the phrase out loud without wincing," replied Kathy, a conservative woman in every sense of the word, fanning herself with vigor.

"I think Eleanor would like it," Brooke said.

"You're probably right," Kathy agreed.

They fell into a companionable silence. Easy, comfortable, and practiced.

Their relationship began on the first day they saw the Beaufort Estate. They had just climbed up the wide circular staircase overlooked by an enormous chandelier, stopping on every floor to take in the varied, ornate layouts. But, when they reached the final stop of the tour, the rooftop terrace railing crumbled, and they nearly fell to their deaths.

Once they'd gotten to safety, the women had exchanged a passing glance of joint relief and utter shock, the first of many sympathetic gestures in the days to come.

A little less than a month later, worried for their safety thanks to fellow contestant Henry—whose father Eleanor had murdered long ago—they conspired in the attic and joined forces. Together, they won the mansion and the generous endowment—their joint merit and plan for the estate were irresistible to Eleanor.

Although it had been less than a year since Eleanor's lawyer, Andrew, had had them sign on the dotted line, while Henry left in a quiet furry, the women felt as if they had known each other for years. Roommates will do that to you, yes, but this was something more, something that felt predestined—an audacious partnership.

As a cool breeze made the umbrella sway, each woman calmly reflected on Brooke's new favorite phrase and their week ahead, thoroughly enjoying a rare break as the warm July sun evaporated water from their bathing-suit-clad skin.

Kathy hoped using the "Fuck Yes or No" doctrine might make her bolder in leading the art collective. She worried her deep concern and consideration of all possible paths might be misinterpreted by the board of directors as hesitancy. *The collective's first year was too important to its longevity to not take seriously*, she thought.

As Executive Director, she considered herself personally responsible for achieving their mission. For the last two months Kathy had written and re-written the mission statement, tweaking it over and over, considering it, and then changing it again. Ultimately, she provided three options to the board which she shared yesterday by email. If she was pushed to think of it from a "Fuck Yes or No" perspective, though, she admitted to herself she had a favorite—but what if the board liked another better? What would that say about her? Would they lose confidence in her, and move from advisors to dictators?

It was too much of a risk presenting just one option, so her "fuck yes" choice stayed private—at least for now.

Today will be delicious, thought Brooke.

Their post-workout relaxation had given her an appetite, and had her dreaming about the test menu Travis would be presenting to her this afternoon. A mentee of Oliver Durand—Eleanor's beau, and former head chef of the Beaufort Estate, not to mention French pastry extraordinaire—Brooke anticipated a decadent, croissant-flaked menu. She hoped her "Fuck Yes" ideology would help her keep each menu short, but somehow she doubted it.

For now, she knew with certainty that this fitness club was a huge fuck yes, and the guests who were scheduled to stay at the

Beaufort Hotel and Art Collective following the grand opening would think so too.

Begrudgingly, Brooke sat up and checked the time on her phone. Just thirty-five minutes left.

"It's almost time. We should head to the locker room and get ready," she said, startling Kathy who had begun to nod off. Playtime was over.

While they were there to exercise and relax by the pool, they also intended to negotiate a collaboration. For the pair, work and play often went hand in hand.

2 JUST US

The Equinox Pro Club was an elite fitness and social club that comprised the top three floors of a high-rise just off Hudson Square. Premium fitness amenities, personal trainers, and spa services catered to celebrities and affluent socialites who craved anonymity.

In the locker room, Brooke shimmied into a violet pencil skirt while studying how Kathy used her ring and pinky fingers to gingerly apply a complimentary anti-aging serum. Now in her mid-thirties, Brooke had a lot to learn from Kathy, whose skin had a youthful glow and whose demeanor was always calm, cool, and collected. The women were opposite in many ways, but both made a pointed effort to be sensitive to differing opinions and points of view.

Kathy relied on Brooke for what she called a gut check—Brooke's reassurance that no, she wasn't crazy for thinking that, or yes, it was a great idea—helped Kathy move forward when she hesitated, which was often. In Brooke's ever-present quest to quell worry, she often pulled Kathy aside to work through her list of pros and cons until, thanks to Kathy's calm nature and sage advice, the right choice became clear, and the weight of the decision was lightened by half.

Things were not always so easy, however, because their core values did not align. Brooke was eager to help anyone and everyone, a trait Kathy found both endearing and naïve, as it necessitated she point out the potential consequences. No, she could not give out leftover food at night to local vagrants, as it would encourage laziness and, in time, attract the kind of crowd that would scare away both hotel guests and members of the art collective, for example. Kathy had traditional values and fought for their security guards to be able to carry loaded weapons, which Brooke eventually relented to—months later admitting she slept better at night knowing they were safe.

The two women were often yin and yang, cordially bringing forward different points of view and talking through them together. In a world filled with polarization and hate, showing kindness and consideration for each other's differences brought the two women even closer together.

In the locker room, Kathy brushed her hair, cleaned out her hairbrush, and pulled back her shoulder-length chestnut-brown and silver hair into a neat ponytail at the base of her neck. Next, she dabbed cream concealer under her eyes, attempting to hide her lack of sleep after a night spent tossing and turning.

Kathy couldn't help but think Brooke was reaching for the stars in approaching this club. She anticipated that exclusivity might be both the appeal for Brooke and the sticking point for the owner. The club was home to the who's who of New York—why should they take a gamble on Brooke's hotel guests? It was a big risk for them, with only a small benefit of a few extra guests per month—but she kept these thoughts to herself. Brooke had surprised her before, and it could happen again. Who was she to tell her not to try?

Kathy stood by Brooke and waited silently while checking her email. Satisfied that her long blonde hair was straightened to professional perfection, Brooke looked at her reflection in the mirror and went into her confidence routine. Tall posture, chin up, hands on hips, shoulders back, deep breath—in through the nose, out through the mouth—and internally chanted, *I can do hard things!*

With an affirmative nod, Kathy acknowledged Brooke's routine was complete, and the dynamic duo turned together toward the double doors that led to the high-ceiling entryway nearest the elevators.

"Brooke Johnson and Kathy Norrwell to see Mr. Aetos," Brooke announced confidently to the woman at the front desk.

Cindy, as her silver name badge displayed, was so immaculately groomed and made-up that she could have been a model for a social media face filter.

"Is anyone else joining you?" Cindy asked automatically.

It was a common question when Brooke and Kathy had a business meeting with a powerful executive. Even if it was subconscious, people expected a man to join them for the meeting. This reality had frustrated Brooke at first, but then she decided to be flattered and respond with all the audacity that polite society could bear.

"Just us," she said with a knowing smirk and a twinkle in her eye.

Cindy soon realized her error and gave the women a mega-watt smile, wordlessly cheering them on while escorting them into the tidy office.

Mr. Aetos had yet to arrive, so Cindy kindly offered Brooke and Kathy water, coffee, or tea, as they lowered themselves into two matching cream swivel chairs that faced a white oak desk in the foreground, and a breathtaking view of the Upper West Side in the background.

As soon as they had the room to themselves, the partners swooned.

"Oh my god, you can see the Hudson River, the Freedom Tower, *and* the Statue of Liberty from here! Unbelievable. The rent on this place must be outrageous," Brooke remarked, unable to tear her eyes away from the view.

"Do you play golf?" asked Kathy, snapping Brooke back to reality. She then noticed several golf trophies in a simple glass case in the corner.

"Hmm, no I don't, but I guess he must. Could be a good angle," Brooke said, and they discussed how something golf-related could sweeten the deal.

A few minutes later, they were startled when a striking man entered the room.

Ronan Sebastian Aetos rushed into his office and shut the door while somehow maintaining a calm demeanor, despite having moved nonstop from one thing to the next all morning. Seeing Brooke and Kathy waiting, he remembered their meeting and wordlessly pivoted back the way he came, requesting Cindy bring him lunch in thirty minutes. He then closed the door a second time with a loud thud, and moved to sit behind his white desk.

Brooke had assumed they would have an hour, and made a mental note that she would need to be extremely succinct. The man's icy demeanor made Kathy very nervous—a feeling she hadn't had from a man since her abusive ex-husband. It was exciting and terrifying at the same time, and she could feel her chest begin to pound as she fought the urge to run. She reminded herself that Brooke was leading this meeting, and she was only there to emphasize their goals, but everything she was thinking came to a complete halt the moment Mr. Aetos sat down and introduced himself. Kathy's lips parted of their own accord when his brown eyes met hers.

Keeping his gaze on Kathy, the former athlete said, "Ladies, I understand we are to discuss a potential collaboration. Could you please introduce yourselves and tell me what you had in mind?"

Brooke looked at Kathy, who was fully ensnared and openly staring at the muscular older man, and spoke up quickly to cover for her.

"Thank you, Mr. Aetos, for meeting with us."

"Please call me Sebastian," he interrupted, before turning his attention to Brooke and offering her a movie-star smile.

"Okay then, Sebastian. I'm Brooke Johnson, and this is Kathy Norrwell. We own the Beaufort Estate—you know, the old mansion that's being renovated on the corner of Fifth Avenue…"

A scowl crossed his face as he quickly rapped his knuckles on his desk. "Oh yes. I think my car was caught in your construction traffic last week," he replied sternly.

This was not going as Brooke had hoped. Her jaw strained as she re-established her smile, faking the positivity required for this important meeting. Without a fitness facility, the Beaufort could never be five-star, and the marketing campaign she had spent the last six months devising would be irrelevant.

"Yes, so sorry about that—the plumbing update went all the way to the middle of the street. Luckily that's over now. In fact, the reason we have been renovating is that we're transforming the property into a boutique five-star hotel and art collective…and that's where I hope you come in." Brooke paused, gauging Sebastian's interest.

"Me? Unless you're planning to host the CrossFit Open, I'm not sure what you mean," he scoffed.

His response was far from ideal, but that's all Brooke had to work with. Kathy nodded encouragement, and Brooke pitched her ideas with all the enthusiasm she could muster.

For the next twenty minutes, Brooke talked nearly nonstop, explaining the similarities between their clientele, the need for a fitness location for their guests, the potential additional revenue Equinox could earn, and how they could collaborate on weddings and large-scale events. Sebastian listened intently, but gave nothing away.

When Brooke finally stopped for air, the muscular man took a moment to assess Brooke, then politely replied, "You've given me a lot to think about. Tell you what, Cindy will give you both a platinum member card for the next thirty days, and I encourage you to stop by our events. I want you to understand who our clients are, and if your hotel guests would mesh well with them. That, and potential capacity issues, are my main concerns at this juncture."

Brooke agreed that was fair. *It's not a no,* she told herself. They shared handshakes and niceties before heading outside and then into the subway, northbound toward the baroque home they had come to love.

3 FOOD FOR THOUGHT

Tabitha the cat greeted Brooke as she stepped out of her room onto the cream runner sitting atop a newly polished wood floor. Her room was one of the few in the estate that she had not touched since Eleanor's mysterious departure with Oliver, nearly a year before. Almost all the other spaces in the estate had been completely remodeled. Brooke had begrudgingly collaborated with contractors to do the necessary updates—like adding electrics and plumbing to the top floor—and had loved every minute of enacting her vision to make a stunning boutique hotel, room by glorious room.

As she made her way down the hall, she caressed the newly upholstered wall panels lovingly, pleased with how the off-white shade brightened the space, and the warm glow of the lights inlaid in the ceiling made the antique hall feel both classic and modern.

Reaching the banister—one of two that mirrored each other and made their way down into the lofty entryway—Brooke recalled the many hours it had taken a crew of six to sand and refinish the wood railing. *Totally worth it*, she thought, as Tabitha trotted eagerly behind her.

At the bottom of the staircase, her modest high heels clicked loudly and reverberated in the cavernous space, dampened only by the lush sofas and leather chairs that they'd brought in to create a cozy hotel lobby. Unable to help herself, Brooke straightened a pillow as she walked by, on her way to take care of a quick errand. Her little brother's birthday had been the day before and she had gotten him a card and slipped two hundred-dollar-bills inside; money seemed to be one of the few gifts teenagers really appreciated. Dropping the envelope into the chute, Brooke couldn't help but worry about her brother. He hadn't been the same since their dad died last year and seemed to turn inward to himself, living in the bright and exciting world of video games while avoiding the real world as much as possible. Or at least that's what her mom had told her—but she was justifiably skeptical about anything her mom told her. God, her mother, Brooke was thankful that there were abundant therapists in Manhattan.

With determination, she refocused her thoughts away from family and back to the task at hand as she reached the three small steps that led from the foyer down into what used to be the servants' quarters.

As Brooke arrived in the English Basement, Travis was carefully moving a silver tray from the counter to the table a few feet away. This kitchen had been Oliver's domain for nearly four decades, long before Travis or Brooke arrived here—that is, until he followed Eleanor off to travel the world.

Brooke noticed the cat tracking of every movement of the tray, as had Travis.

"Sorry, Tabby. I'll give you scraps if there's any left," the chef said to Tabitha, who then sauntered off down the hall.

Brooke's stomach had growled audibly the moment she arrived in the kitchen, the smell of browned butter deliciously filling the air.

"You knew I was rooting for you all along, didn't you?" Travis asked Brooke.

"No, I didn't know that," she admitted modestly.

During the contest to win the estate, five people had competed fiercely—all the while, Travis had dutifully appeared impartial, just as Eleanor had directed.

"Yup, I was secretly rooting for you to win the estate, and then I was shocked to learn that both you and Kathy had won together. I didn't even realize that was an option. Did you?"

"Well, we kind of had no choice. We needed to combine our business plans because Henry seemed...unhinged, to say the least. Honestly, it was the safest thing to do. I'm just glad she went for it," Brooke admitted.

Travis had been slow to warm up to Kathy after they started working together. Each time he offered her a nicety, she seemed to shy away or become defensive, but after witnessing this on several occasions with other people, he realized she was simply cautious.

Brooke and Travis's friendship, on the other hand, had come fast and furious.

In the two minutes she so skillfully extracted Eleanor's whereabouts from him, before storming off to the hospital, Travis knew Brooke was a force of nature and felt incredibly intimidated by her. Now, after several months of working together to build the hotel's restaurant, they had all fallen into a rhythm and an easy friendship.

Stomach growling, Brooke approached Travis at the butcher block dining table, a space that doubled as a pastry prep station in the wee hours of the morning. Two neat place settings hugged the corner of the table, along with gray-lavender cloth napkins, bright white plates, and modern brass silverware. A test sample, and identical to the place settings that Brooke and Travis had placed a bulk order for last week.

"Please sit, Brooke," Travis instructed happily as he motioned to the chair, wiping his hands on the front of his white button-up apron.

Brooke was at ease as Travis hovered over her, basking in the smell of fresh baked goods, but it was then she realized Travis was nervous—and that made her nervous.

What if the menu was not what she had envisioned? What if she didn't like the food?

She reminded herself that he was not just any hired chef; he was hand-selected and apprenticed by Oliver. He had been working at the estate for years on special occasions, serving celebrities and elite socialites. Before leaving, Eleanor had ensured that Travis had been paid handsomely to help Brooke and Kathy launch the restaurant within the hotel…but how embarrassing would it be for him if she didn't think he could cut it? Not to mention she would have to fire him. *God, she would hate that.*

Travis watched as Brooke carefully surveyed the table full of elegantly plated meals, returned Travis's smile, pushed her trepidation aside, and simply asked, "Where should we begin?"

"Today, I've prepared appetizers and brunch," he began formally. "These menus are critical to profitability because they allow people to sample the food quality, and then if they like the dishes, they will come back at dinner. Especially in a hotel format. Guests will be hungry in the morning and between meals, even if they didn't plan on dining here."

Brooke listened as he explained his restaurant program and

marketing approach for what would become The Beaufort Hotel and Art Collective. She kept her face supportive and neutral, yet he was filled with angst—he was rambling, going on an energetic rant for a full ten minutes. Brooke was sure it was just the excitement of it all, but the food was getting cold.

Noticing her raised eyebrows, Travis stopped speaking abruptly. A departure from the formal etiquette she was trying to adopt now that her life was one surrounded by a more affluent crowd, Brooke leaned forward on the table, rested her chin on her hand, and gave Travis a wide smile. Sensing his uncertainty, she simply teased him by asking the same question again. "Where should we begin?"

Exhaling while shaking his head at himself, he looked embarrassed but also happy. Brooke had not objected to any of his ideas—in fact, she was pleased he was being so thoughtful about the hotel menu.

Travis quickly pulled forward a bowl-like plate from the end of the table and took a seat, sliding the dish between them. "Go for it. The eggs are probably cold already. Sorry, I was on a bit of a roll there."

Brooke picked up her silverware and went straight for the center of the bowl, which was filled with creamy eggs, yolks still intact, and smoked salmon.

Travis interrupted her before she was finished scooping, "Oh no, allow me." He then took the fork directly out of her hand, launching into an explanation of the dish and how he wanted her to get the perfect bite, all the while meticulously loading up her fork.

Brooke thought he was being silly or perhaps controlling—either way, this was his show, and she wanted to see it play out.

Travis watched carefully as the perfect bite slipped past Brooke's nude pink lips.

The bite was everything Brooke had dreamt it would be, and she closed her eyes and moaned, unable to stop herself. Realizing how ridiculous she must look, she quickly opened them and caught Travis staring at her mouth, earnest delight on his face.

Their moment of mutual satisfaction was interrupted when Tabitha reappeared and jumped onto the kitchen counter. Cats are jealous creatures, and Tabitha was no exception.

With a concerted effort, Travis peeled his eyes away from Brooke's lips and went back to business. He discussed the ingredients, cost, and margins for each dish they tried.

Brooke listened intently as he explained that the margins were tight in the restaurant business. Between the food costs and the staff, the restaurant may not be profitable for a year, perhaps two. The only redeeming quality, Travis explained, was that alcoholic beverages could be very profitable—highball cocktails often have an eighty percent margin, for example. Brooke nodded eagerly at that and plotted how she could push cocktails at every opportunity.

Next, Travis presented Brooke with a spreadsheet of costs: cleaning and inspection of the hood, fire safety necessities, cutlery and dishes, commercial appliances, and containers and restaurant supplies that needed to be stocked. He explained that every item would need to be in order before the state health inspector came to visit and that they would likely need to have a second inspection before opening.

This is terrifying, Brooke thought while trying desperately to conceal her concerns. Travis paused, and she realized then that he was waiting for her to say something. Wide-eyed, Brooke mumbled, "I'm not sure what all this means…I just…I can't believe we won't be profitable for a year."

Travis apologized with a shrug, explaining that it was just the nature of the restaurant business.

Unsure what to do, Brooke gave him a curt smile and took the sheet of expenses in her hand before abruptly leaving the English Basement the same way she came.

4 KATHY

"Do we have a quorum?" Kathy asked at 3:02 p.m.

"No, we're still waiting on a few others," replied the board secretary.

Kathy gave a slight nod as she sat at the head of the table, visible from the art gallery space on the first floor of the estate, finally embracing her power.

For the first several board meetings, she felt herself an imposter, as she often had throughout her life. Once, when she was eight, her mother noticed how studious she was and encouraged her to teach her brothers the advanced math she had learned in her honors class. She was elated, and then equally crushed when they relentlessly made fun of her. They told her she was stupid, interrupted her when she spoke, and told her to keep quiet.

Even at eight, Kathy realized they were echoing the same phrases and behavior her father had normalized toward her mother. It was then she reasoned, that was just how the world worked for women. From that moment on, she turned inward, finding solace in staying silent. She became soft-spoken and meek in most instances and also very lonely, lacking affection at home and camaraderie at school. She knew she was missing out, but considered it a small price to pay to avoid confrontation.

Now, at last—at nearly fifty years of age—she felt grounded. She was where she should be at the head of the boardroom table. She adjusted her posture while looking out into the art gallery through the floor-to-ceiling windows that made up the fourth wall of the conference room, and idly wondered if this was how men felt their entire lives. *Yes, probably so*, she concluded.

Kathy decided then and there she was not going backward. No more cowering, no more staying silent when she had something of value to say, no more interruptions.

The remaining board members trickled in and sat along the three off-white walls of the boardroom, the same as the simple white table. The only colorful things in the room were the people, an intentional choice so as not to detract attention from the gallery.

Kathy was among eight board members and one guest—all varying in age and levels of flamboyance.

"We now have a quorum, Ms. Norrwell," Joan informed her.

"Very good. Thank you all for coming today. Given it is our fourth board meeting, I invited a guest—which, you will notice, I added to the agenda," Kathy announced to the group and, with a sense of pride previously unthinkable, she began passing out paper copies of it. Shortly, a motion to approve it was made by Maddox Frankfort, and seconded by Anabelle Westerbelt.

With that out of the way, Kathy began the meeting by introducing her guest.

Gregory Michael Blottingham the Third was well-regarded in art and finance circles alike—he likely needed no introduction, but it would be rude not to do so. A jovial man in his early fifties, Greg possessed a winning combination of authenticity, grandeur, and likeability—a rare set of traits that only money can buy. As Kathy read his short bio to the board members, she was pleased she had nurtured this relationship over the years, and hoped it would cement her reputation with the burgeoning board. Hard to tell, though, as the board members simply nodded and offered polite comments of welcome.

The rest of the board meeting proceeded as planned, with committee chairs giving their reports. The finance committee gave an overview of the budget and P&L, then provided projections and announced that, with the art sale last month and incoming memberships, the organization was off to a good start. The membership chair named eleven new art collective members, while the volunteer core had recruited two new volunteer docents. The selection committee had already identified the artists and live events to be performed during the upcoming grand opening and gave a short update on each, save one. There was a surprise being planned. Kathy did not like that at all—being in control kept her sane, safe, and calm. Kept her anxiety at bay.

Focusing on what she *could* control, Kathy told the board she would like to show a painting from the Beaufort Collection at the event—and held up a copy of it. Then, the question Kathy had been avoiding came to a head.

"That's incredible!" Cynthia remarked. Looking around the table, Kathy realized the shock on the other board members' faces mirrored Cynthia's.

She continued, "Where on earth did you get an original pastel on paper Degas? Are those kinds of works here? What else is in the Beaufort Collection? I feel like if we knew what we had, we could do any number of things."

It was a valid question, and Kathy certainly had many ideas about what they could do. However, what she didn't want people to know was that a priceless collection of art was currently leaning up against the rafters in the attic. Not only would they be rightfully appalled at the conditions the art was being kept in, but it could also pose a security risk.

"Great question. Yes, the Beaufort Estate owns several prized works, many of which are in rotation in galleries throughout the world," Kathy answered subtly suggesting the art was not there —a half-truth. She quickly continued, "I would love to hear your ideas about what we can do. Even if the Beaufort Estate does not possess a particular piece that you would consider relevant to an event, I could make some calls given the relationships I'm building with curators."

Deflection complete, Kathy quickly moved on to the next item on the agenda—and to her delight, no other dicey questions were asked of her. Still, for the duration of the meeting, her plans for how to secure the estate distracted her.

Once the final committee member had spoken, and no other business remained, Kathy closed the meeting and turned to her guest.

"Greg, is now still a good time for you?" she asked.

"Yes, I have around thirty minutes," Greg replied, eager to get to what he had come for.

After the last board member left the room, Kathy began her

scheduled tour with Greg. A man of both generational wealth and intelligent investing, he had committed to be a major gift donor for the collective and was interested in pieces from the Beaufort Collection for his summer home. Kathy had spoken about the Degas specifically to ensure he stayed through what he may otherwise have felt was a mundane meeting—whetting his appetite for what was to come.

Exiting the glass-encased room to the gallery, Kathy led Greg left to what looked more and more like a sophisticated combination of the Ritz Paris and The Standard hotel lobbies. Light turquoise velvet sofas were positioned next to high-back, well-worn leather chairs, with polished concrete end tables beside them. Three large traditional chandeliers glowed above in a line, centered within the tin ceiling tiles, providing the space with ample glowing light. The paintings on the walls were each carefully lit with brass picture lights.

Kathy was delighted at how Brooke had transformed the space from quiet-traditional into a vibrant mix of textures and colors, while keeping the space timeless. It was something she could never have imagined, yet it worked so well. Looking at Greg, she could tell he also approved as he whistled a low, singular note while slowly pivoting around the grand foyer.

Kathy began up the stairs, but paused when she realized Greg was no longer following her—something had caught his attention.

5 BROOKE

Reaching the top step within the foyer, Brooke paused and took a deep breath. She told herself the money was not a big deal and that the estate was already well funded, but emotionally, she was devastated.

Kathy was already turning a profit, and she was hemorrhaging money. *What kind of partner did that?* She wondered if Kathy had even realized how much she was spending, and if she had begun harboring resentment towards her. Did she think she was irresponsible? Was Kathy working so diligently to turn a profit so that she could rightfully conclude Brooke was not successful, and then ask her to bow out of the partnership? Was her failure to make money causing Kathy to lose trust in her? Once you've worried about money for so long, it becomes difficult to stop—like any habit, Brooke reasoned with herself, attempting to stop the spiral of negativity.

Determined to rise above, she decided to give herself a moment of stillness right there in the arch between the English Basement and the foyer. Brooke closed her eyes and thought, *I can do hard things.*

When her eyelids flicked open, she had the uncanny feeling of being watched, and immediately scanned the room before her—expecting to see Tabitha. Instead, at the foot of the main staircase, which curved upward, she saw an older man to whom Kathy was speaking. He had a shock of dark brown hair that was graying at the sides, just above his ears. With a smile that showed his dimples, a tailored suit, and shined shoes, he was looking directly at her—unabashed.

Unused to such attention, Brooke glanced behind her to check if Travis had followed her, and if the man could be looking at Travis. He hadn't, and he wasn't.

Realizing the man must be Kathy's friend, Brooke reluctantly smiled and gave a brief wave. The visitor's face lit up tenderly. He seemed kind. Brooke then moved across the room to greet him.

Extending an arm as Brooke approached, Kathy said, "Gregory, this is my business partner, Brooke Johnson. She's responsible for the gorgeous renovation and all things related to the hotel and restaurant."

"Very impressive, Miss Johnson," Gregory replied.

"And Brooke, this is Gregory Blottingham the Third. He was kind enough to attend a board meeting and now I'm giving him a tour of our private art collection," Kathy added, with a particular look that Brooke knew to mean he was a wealthy donor and to give them a wide berth.

Brooke had learned a while ago that Kathy worked best when she was not nearby. Despite her exceptional résumé, Kathy's feelings of inadequacy presented themselves in varied ways, and often enough Brooke had come to recognize and attempt to reverse them. Kathy could spend an hour trying to select her outfit for the day, picking something, deciding against it and so on, until there were more clothes on the floor than on hangers.

Eventually, Kathy came to Brooke for help—and now it happened several times a week. At first, Brooke assumed she didn't understand color theory, but that wasn't it—she was into art, after all. Brooke also noticed that, when in small groups of three or four, Kathy would allow the others to dominate the conversation, and she became exceedingly polite. After several months, the theme became apparent: Kathy often didn't trust herself and valued other people's opinions more than her own.

Brooke was determined to help her get out of her own way.

With a head tilt, Gregory asked, "And Brooke, will you be joining us for the tour?" His hand hovered a few inches from her lower back, his body language subtly encouraging her to step up the stairs with them.

"Oh no, I have a meeting in a few minutes, I'm afraid," Brooke said, taking a small step sideways. It was a clumsy lie, but she was still uncomfortable around wealthy people and felt put on the spot—not to mention the warmth radiating from his hand was unnerving.

Just then, Travis trotted up from the English Basement. Brooke used the sound of his shoes on the marble as a welcome distraction and glanced over her shoulder. He appeared amused by the exchange, waved casually, and continued by to what would become the restaurant passthrough and coffee bar.

While Gregory looked at Travis, Brooke's focus snapped to Kathy and implored action with wide, "help-me" eyes. Taking the cue, Kathy spoke up, reminding Gregory how little time they had, and how much she had to show him. He gave in then and turned up the stairs to follow Kathy, giving Brooke a final wink.

Brooke shook her head to herself, with a smirk on her face. *That was...flattering*, she thought. She then wondered how much Kathy would make for the estate from a private sale to that gentleman. As the familiar feeling of guilt settled over her, Brooke scrunched her face up and went to the private seating area in the new restaurant, determined to get some much-needed perspective.

When Eleanor picked up the phone, a wave of relief moved through Brooke's muscles. She was now comfortably seated in a leather booth.

"Hello dear, to what do I owe the pleasure?" Eleanor asked Brooke.

"I'm so sorry to bother you, Eleanor, but I'm kind of struggling here. I'm in my own head and I was hoping you might have some advice to share," admitted Brooke.

"Of course, that's what I'm here for. And don't apologize, for heaven's sake. Women need to stop saying sorry all the time—especially when we have nothing to be sorry about."

"Yes, you're right. It's a bad habit, I guess. I'll add it to my list," Brooke said with a quick huff.

"So what's troubling you?"

"Well, Kathy has been doing amazing. She set up a board for the collective, sold a painting, and put another in a museum. She's already profitable, and me...well, I'm burning through money. I just don't know if I'm cut out for this," Brooke said sadly.

Straight to the point, Eleanor asked, "Is the endowment still operational?"

"Yes."

"Are you going over budget on all the items?"

"No, not all, just some, and they have been big ones. The

renovations have just been really expensive," Brooke admitted sheepishly.

"They usually are. That's just the nature of renovating an ancient building. So, is that it?"

"No, the restaurant is burning money too. And the other day, Travis told me it's unlikely to be profitable for a *year, possibly two!* I just…feel guilty. Like I'm blowing it. Kathy's already profitable, and there's no profit in sight for either the hotel or the restaurant. I don't know if this will really work," Brooke said, tears now flowing down her cheeks.

Then, out of the blue, Travis handed her a napkin and left promptly.

I must look like an absolute mess, Brooke thought while dabbing her eyes.

"Brooke, listen to me carefully. I realize you didn't grow up with much, and because of that, you may want to see success happen quickly. It's a good trait, except when it's not. This is one of those times that it's not. You are building something meaningful and worthwhile, and those kinds of endeavors take time. I know you can do this—that's why I chose you," said Eleanor.

"Yeah?" Brooke asked, studying the details on the wooden table in front of her, longing for reassurance.

"Yes, without a doubt. You haven't even launched the hotel yet. Of course you wouldn't be making a profit. Just be patient with yourself and keep at it."

"Yes, yes, okay. You're right, of course. Thank you for answering, Eleanor. You're the best," said Brooke.

"Yes, and don't you forget it. Au revoir, darling. Give 'em hell."

"Thanks," Brooke said with a sigh, hanging up.

"Well, that was endearing."

Brooke snapped to attention, surprised to see her mother standing there with a tight smile on her face.

"Uh, hi. Hi! Hi? What are you doing here, Mom?"

"Oh, you know, I thought I'd come by and see you and how your whole hotel thing was going. Now, come give your mama a hug!" Alice said with dramatic enthusiasm, opening her arms in expectation.

Brooke took the cue and embraced her with reservation. Stepping back, she said, "I'm just so surprised. I thought you were living on the coast with a boyfriend. And how did you even get in here?" she asked, looking around the restaurant and out to the lobby, both utterly devoid of people.

"Through the door, of course. I knocked and the cute cook let me in. You looked like you were making an important call, so I waited patiently for a few minutes."

Brooke knew that meant she was actively eavesdropping on what must have been the entire conversation. She hoped she hadn't said anything her mother could dig into. It's not that she didn't love her mother; it was just that the woman could somehow be both too much and not enough at the same time.

"As for living on the coast, I was and am. My guy has some business uptown for a month or so, so I joined him and thought I'd come see you. Who were you talking to just now?" she asked with a tone of innocence Brooke knew to be a ruse.

"Eleanor, the previous owner of the estate. She acts as an advisor—it's written into the endowment terms."

In reality, talking with Eleanor was completely optional, but Brooke said it in an attempt to quell the jealousy she knew her mother was harboring.

"What about Eddie?" Brooke asked, concerned for her little brother, moving the spotlight away from herself.

"Oh, he's staying with the neighbor kid. They're good friends now, both seniors in the same high school. He prefers playing video games at all hours of the night rather than hanging out with dear ol' mom. So I figured, why not travel a bit?"

Unbelievable, she thought. *I had a strictly enforced nine p.m. bedtime until I left the house. No way in hell would she have let me stay with some neighbor's kid let alone play games all night.*

That was logical Brooke thinking, and while it was true — she knew her frustration stemmed from much more than logic.

Her mother had always been somewhat unstable and to expect anything less was just credulous, something Brooke didn't realize fully until therapy. Perhaps she was still discovering the extent of her misplaced optimism.

The first time she realized something was not right was when her mother insisted on walking her to middle school, something she never did, and cried nearly the whole way. It was a strange walk. Mom was overly clingy, and Brooke, a nine-year-old with appropriately aged emotional maturity, had no idea what to say or do, so they walked. Mom asked weird questions while she attempted to answer them without upsetting her more, looking anywhere else than her mom's face to avoid the complete devastation rubbing off on her. That day when she returned home from school her mother was gone; taken to a recovery hospital for a nervous breakdown. Something no one wanted to explain or talk about. She had been quietly devastated, trying to hold it together for her brother's sake.

There were many other times, most not as stark, but just as full of emotional landmines. Thankfully, Brooke had come to terms with most of her past involving her mother, as the relevant concepts were neatly explained by a very patient professional. Generational trauma, the Karpman Drama Triangle, and *hooray* Cognitive Behavioral Therapy to the rescue!

After her father's death just over a year ago, Brooke's mom had mourned for a few months and then seemed to turn into another person altogether. This was not surprising in hindsight, but it was shocking at the time. Brooke's formerly reserved mother—the same person who clung to religion and refused to let her listen to the hip-hop radio station—had started going to nightclubs and drinking way too much. And, to make matters worse, she would call her at all hours of the night to tell her just how exciting it was. Brooke was thrown off balance by the hypocrisy of it all. At one point, she confided in her grandmother and learned that her mother had been diagnosed as bipolar as a kid, a fact that would have been incredibly helpful about twenty years prior. Now, Mom stood in front of her with no warning, yet still expectant of Brooke's care and congeniality. *She was her mother, after all.*

Deciding not to derail her day completely, she let her mom off the hook and simply replied, "Oh, cool. He must like that." While it was true that her brother was likely in video game heaven, she also felt guilty that her brother was enduring so much change.

Alice insisted on staying at the estate for a few nights. She reasoned that she could give Brooke the same feedback as a guest would.

While the offer was indeed practical, and she wanted feedback, Brooke was vibrating with irritation. Giving in, she led her mother to one of the guest rooms while telling her how busy she was for the rest of the day, insisting she had no time for socializing.

6 HENRY

On that final day, when the winner of the contest was announced, Eleanor's lawyer had strong-armed Henry into signing the concession paperwork—the terms of which barely stopped short of a restraining order.

"Watch yourself, asshole!" a delivery driver on a green and white scooter shouted, as Henry nearly bumped him while trying to avoid some metal scaffolding that covered the façade of an older building.

"Oh fuck off!" Henry replied to the guy's backpack as he sped off unharmed. Was it just him, or were New Yorkers getting even more aggressive? No matter, he thought, letting his mind wander back to the Beaufort Estate contest.

The last year had been a slap in the face, and it was all because of the estate. The estate and that bitch, Eleanor—a woman who disguised her narcissism as altruism. The murderer bequeathed her legacy to two women, Brooke and Kathy, rather than someone who was actually qualified to receive it. Architecture, after all, was *his* thing. Or it had been, anyway. That was before he was fired from his position at the firm and ridiculed within the industry.

After the business plan exercise, Eleanor asked all three remaining contestants—Brooke, Kathy, and Henry—to begin making connections that might help them execute their plans. Henry had been so certain he would win that he not only called on his professional connections, but also started making arrangements. He was trying to be proactive, and look where that got him. The firm he worked for considered his negotiations with the property developer moonlighting and grounds for termination, even though he didn't actually win the estate. He was fired and left with no income, a very pissed-off developer, and a bad reputation in the industry—a reputation he had spent thirty years building ruined overnight.

Not only that, his plans to divorce his wife with a proverbial middle finger had been dashed. After he signed the estate paperwork and gathered his things, he went back to their condo in Brooklyn and had to explain to her what happened. He had planned that, after winning the estate, he would go to his lawyer to draw up divorce papers and have them served immediately. Timing was key. He needed to divorce her before the mansion was transferred to him legally, so that he could use the $70 million estate to fund the demolition and put up his portion of cash for the construction of a new high rise. She would be left with the measly value of half of their house, and then would soon find out he had become incredibly wealthy without her.

But no, losing the estate to Brooke and Kathy ruined all that.

Instead of going to the lawyer to draw up the divorce paperwork as he had planned, Henry went with a highly defensible directive informing him never to step foot inside the estate, or come near Brooke or Kathy again. He then had to go home to his wife empty-handed and explain that he didn't win the contest. She asked annoying questions, and he avoided her for as long as possible, until he couldn't take it anymore. He filed for divorce and lost half of everything he had worked for his entire life, and now paid alimony to a bitch who had cheated on him. All because of Brooke and Kathy—two women who did not deserve the estate.

He deserved it. Eleanor had killed his father—it was only fair, only *right*—that he was bequeathed it to him. He suspected, too, that Brooke had figured out it was Eleanor, and guessed that she had used that fact against him to win the contest. That girl was always meddling in other people's business—and she had acted strangely toward him in the end. He was owed something, and Eleanor was long gone, enjoying her newfound freedom.

He had hoped Brooke and Kathy would have reached out to him to include him somehow, but they hadn't, so he began assiduously following their social media profiles. Brooke and Kathy posted very little on their personal accounts, but the estate had been rebranded as the Beaufort Hotel and Art Collective. The photos, he had to admit, looked stunning. The pair were living high on the hog while Henry dipped into his retirement savings to cover everyday expenses. It was ridiculous. It gutted him to watch his plans for retirement get farther and farther away. Something needed to be done, and fast.

Reaching Bird & Branch, he pulled open the door and stepped into the white-and-gray hipster café, complete with hexagon-shaped tables and too many plants.

"Thanks for meeting me here," said Henry, reaching for his former colleague's hand.

"Sure," Hugo said nervously, "would you mind if we went for a walk in Central Park? I'm overcaffeinated already."

"Absolutely. It's a lovely day for it," Henry replied, knowing all too well that Hugo was making an excuse—he didn't want them to be seen together, and Henry couldn't blame him.

"So, how are things? Have you found another architecture firm?" the tall man with blond curly hair asked him directly.

"I'm still looking. Trying to be selective," Henry clarified in an attempt to preserve what little there was left of his reputation. In truth, Henry had been applying everywhere, digging out his old Rolodex to find people who hadn't heard he'd been fired.

"Makes sense—you've been in the business a long time," said the younger man. "Any leads?" Then, after looking from left to right, he added quietly, "I'm looking too, although a bit more casually. Don't tell anyone, of course."

"Secret's safe with me," Henry assured him. "No major prospects at the moment," he said confidently, knowing that if he had a lead, he certainly wouldn't be sharing it with anyone.

"What about dating? I heard you finally got a divorce."

"Oh yes, thank the lord for that. We are officially divorced, and everything's been split up. I have a small apartment in Hell's Kitchen. But yes, I am dating. It's nice to have a meal with someone who likes you," he joked dryly.

Hugo humored him and chuckled. "Anyone interesting?"

"Not really, more of a means to an end. She's fun to be around. It's nice to flirt again, you know?" he said, trying to step out of the spotlight.

"I know what you mean. Things can be a bit dry day to day with Lucy. But we still love each other. And the kids are young, so there's that. Where's your girl now?"

"She's not from here, so she's out seeing the museums and

visiting friends for a few days. I met her upstate."

"Ah, I see. So more of a fling then?"

"Exactly," Henry confirmed.

The men continued to walk and talk for a while longer, and when a natural break came, Henry took it. The meeting was pleasant, but altogether unsuccessful, garnering no job leads.

He needed to do something to earn money, and fast.

7 LIES

Kathy was startled by a tapping on the door of the office she and Brooke shared. After the contest had ended, the study had been converted to accommodate two sizeable antique mahogany desks with double computer screens on each, facing back-to-back, and a small seating area for brainstorming meetings or hosting guests. This was a convenient setup—when the partners wanted to talk, they simply leaned around their screens and could look directly at each other.

The knocking couldn't be Brooke, Kathy realized with a start. She never knocked—why would she?

As Kathy swiveled her chair around, she was surprised to find Maddox Frankfort, one of the more accomplished members of the board of directors, standing there. His background was in finance, and he had been the former vice president of a well-known wealth management firm.

She stood from her office chair and shook his hand. "Mr. Frankfort, what a surprise. Welcome, please sit down." Kathy motioned to the small sitting area nearest the balcony room, where she joined him. "What can I do for you?" she asked, bright-eyed.

"Kathy, it isn't good news. I received a strange email today, and I'm afraid I'm not the only one."

"Ah, a mystery then," Kathy said in a chipper tone, not picking up on the seriousness of the situation.

The distinguished man, with prominent jowls and thinning gray hair, continued, "The email was sent from an obviously fake address but was very specific," he said, leaving her in suspense. "You know nothing about it?"

Kathy laughed and shook her head, bewildered. "Absolutely nothing. What are you trying to tell me, Maddox?"

"The letter—well, the email—contains severe allegations against you. Let me pull it up on my phone. You can read it yourself."

He handed Kathy his phone, and an email from yourinformat1923@gmail.com read:

Dear Board Member of The Beaufort Hotel and Art Collective,

I wanted to inform you of the nature of your Executive Director, Kathy Norrwell. I'm a patron of MoMA and have been for years, and it was discovered that while Kathy worked there, she embezzled money from the museum. It was kept quiet at the time, of course, so as not to damage the reputations of many. But now, I feel a duty to tell you. Especially because she is currently selling fraudulent paintings and knockoffs, claiming they are from the Beaufort Collection.

As a distinguished member of society, I couldn't let this go unsaid.

Yours in secrecy,
A fellow art enthusiast.

"Dear god!" Kathy responded, her eyes bulging as she looked at Maddox, wondering if he believed it. "Lies, they are lies! I swear it! How dare someone tarnish my career and reputation," she shouted as the board member watched calmly. "When was this sent? And who all to? Do you know?" she asked him frantically.

"It was sent to all of the board members, and I believe word has gotten out to a few others. I was approached about it. The board selected me to speak to you," he clarified.

"Oh, Oh no…" Kathy's breath escaped her in a deep sigh as she tried to comprehend the far-reaching impact of this poison-pen letter. She braced herself, knowing she must act diplomatically. If she went wild, it would only make Maddox question her character and serve to reinforce the accusations.

"Thank you. Thank you so very much for bringing this to my attention. I assure you my record at MoMA is pristine, and these allegations are completely false. Could you please forward the email to me? I want to inform HR at MoMA, and send a copy to my lawyer to try to get to the bottom of things. It does our collective no good to have such gossip out in the wild. And, perhaps, do you think it would be wise to call an emergency meeting with the board?"

Kathy knew it was a good idea but sought to include the man in her decision-making. He was known to be level-headed—likely why he'd been elected to speak with her.

"Yes, I think that's wise. However, two board members have already submitted their resignation. I encouraged them to wait for your response, but they were adamant that even these accusations may harm their reputation by proximity."

"Unbelievable," muttered Kathy.

"Let me send an email to the remaining board summarizing your response. It's important to have these things documented. I'll send you a copy." With that, he stood and shook her hand.

Kathy went through the motions, still stunned, while he looked at her with pity.

"Thank you. Thank you for coming. We'll get through this," was the best response she could muster.

The gentleman nodded and left quietly.

Kathy sat and thought about the conversation for several minutes, then decided to seek out Brooke. She needed to confide in someone, yes, but this also had the potential to stunt the growth of their business. She needed to tell her partner immediately.

She searched the house, going from room to room. Making her way through the empty English Basement, she came to the final place she knew Brooke liked to go. Dodging the staff staircase, she opened the too-small door to reveal the miniature cube-like courtyard in the center of the house. Travis had developed a robust vegetable and herb garden within the four-by-four square feet of earth, and its contents spilled out onto a small path surrounding it.

That's where Brooke and her mother stood, on the far side of the path, in deep conversation.

"Oh good, I found you," said Kathy, relieved she didn't have to continue her search.

"Yes, I was just showing Mom all the fresh herbs Travis uses in the kitchen."

"Well, I have bad news. Someone put out a nasty lie about me…and it could ruin everything."

Brooke stared as Kathy attempted to rub the numbness out of her hands, not quite knowing how to start explaining this, and how much to say in front of Brooke's mother.

Understanding her partner's reluctance, Brooke quickly made an excuse and left the garden so they could speak alone.

The two women moved upstairs to the lobby, where Kathy gave Brooke the play-by-play of what had just occurred.

"You remember Anabelle Westerbelt—the board member from upstate? Well, she and one other director already resigned. The collective is crumbling!" said Kathy, disbelief and dejection coloring her words. "Everything I've worked so hard for could all be ruined. Do you remember that donor, Gregory, the one you met? Well, if he hears of this, we can kiss that private sale goodbye. If word gets out, everyone will question the entire Beaufort Collection. It's a disaster," she concluded.

"Oh my god. So, what's next? What do we do?" asked Brooke.

"You've got enough on your plate—let me manage this. The next step is an emergency board meeting. I'll be asked about everything, which is fine, except that I'm beside myself. I don't want to fumble this, but I'm so stressed! I've got to call my friend in HR at MoMA. This could be bad for them, too, if it gets out —even though it's not true."

8 EGO

It was networking day for the business partners, and Brooke was excited to get out of the house.

The July sun made the transition from the ornate double doors of the estate to the car unpleasant. Relieved, the women buckled their seat belts in the well-air-conditioned leather interior of the car that Melissa, the chauffeur and head of security, now drove. Hiring Melissa and buying the Volvo was one of the first changes Brooke and Kathy made when they inherited the estate. Eleanor had been spending a small fortune on ride-shares and car services, and they worried about security.

Melissa Franklin was ex-military and was moonlighting as retail store security when they met her. She was looking for stable work, and Brooke and Kathy were looking for a stable woman who believed in their vision. For far too long, their academic success, careers, and overall well-being had all been at the discretion of a man. Women like themselves were hardworking, yet were often underestimated and second-guessed.

It was for this reason they wanted to build a female team—a found family of women who they could trust and rely on. Together, these women were unstoppable. Melissa told it like it was—she drove fast and took care of business. At times, the weight of leadership got to Brooke and Kathy, but they were always at their most relaxed when they were in the car with Melissa behind the wheel. Some of their best moments happened in the car, going from here to there.

Today, Brooke and Kathy had coordinated their schedules to stack two networking events back to back in an unspoken agreement to get away from Brooke's meddling mother, who could often be found talking loudly on her phone in one corner of the estate or another. Brooke had justified this schedule by saying that, if you're going to go to the trouble of dressing to impress and doing your hair and makeup to the nines, you might as well get a few appearances out of it.

Brooke aimed to meet influential people and tell them about the hotel, so that they could book events and encourage visiting relatives to stay there. Meanwhile Kathy hoped to meet artists and wealthy patrons. The women's circles rarely overlapped, and when networking, it was inevitable that one of them would meet someone who would be best in the other's circle, and would thus go out of their way to introduce them. This was women uplifting other women, true, but it was also a smooth handoff, a way to politely exit an otherwise irrelevant conversation.

Shortly after two, they arrived at the exclusive networking event. The elevator opened onto the penthouse suite with a considerable footprint and breathtaking view that looked directly at the Empire State Building. People fluttered next to the window like moths, not quite looking at the view but unable to stay away. With a nod, Brooke and Kathy parted ways.

Brooke grabbed a pre-made cocktail lined up on the counter next to the abundant spread of hors d'oeuvres. She had learned long ago that networking was nearly impossible while eating, but a drink could provide a well-needed pause or excuse to leave a conversation.

Kathy needed no such tool. Years of giving gallery tours gave her immediate confidence and automatic talking points in this setting, and her baseline trepidation vanished. Whatever was on the wall, Kathy could talk about it, and doing so tended to attract the right people.

Brooke struck up a conversation with a man named Kevin, a real estate agent who was building his team. He was obviously trying to recruit Brooke, but she politely demurred and instead told him about the hotel. He assumed she was a hired general manager, as was often the case. Even when she casually mentioned that she owned the estate, it was as if he didn't hear her at all. She wondered if he was hard of hearing, assumed she was lying, or was otherwise in denial.

Brooke decided to drop it in again. "Yes, when Kathy and I were bequeathed the mansion, the task of renovating it into a hotel almost seemed overwhelming…but it's amazing how far it's come."

When networking, the easiest thing to do is ask follow-up questions in direct response to what a person has just shared. When Brooke dropped the fact that she owned the mansion into conversation, the usual responses were, "Oh, and when did that happen?" or "Oh, bequest? Who was the previous owner? I might know them?" That is if she was believed, of course, and she was only believed if the ego of the person she was talking to could handle it. Often, they couldn't. This was the case with the real estate man she was talking to.

Brooke quickly recovered from the awkwardness in the conversation by complimenting him, saying, "If you are expanding your agency, you must be doing well. Tell me, do you have any specialties?"

It was at this point that she actively began zoning him out and listening to the conversations around her, while nodding and politely sipping her cocktail. She glanced over at Kathy and did a double-take.

Kathy looked ashen and visibly swayed while touching the wall and carrying on her conversation. Immediately, Brooke turned back to the man and excused herself, claiming to need to refresh her drink. Worried, she went straight to Kathy, who then used her as an excuse to close her conversation with an art enthusiast politely.

Kathy whispered to Brooke, "Message Melissa to pull up front now, please."

"Are you okay?" asked Brooke.

"No, I don't think so," Kathy replied under her breath. "Something is very wrong."

9 SECRETS

Once back in the car, the two women huddled together in the backseat, seatbelts forgotten. Kathy watched the concern on Brooke's face, as she pivoted her knees across the middle-seat hump and clasped their hands together.

She felt somewhat ashamed, having hidden her symptoms from Brooke and delayed going to the doctor for so long. For women like her—women pushing fifty—these kinds of symptoms were never good news. She feared cancer, as most logical people do—or perhaps she'd had a minor stroke, or possibly an undiagnosed heart condition? Anxiety ran amok when her symptoms set in, fear soaring through the roof. Maybe anxiety was a symptom? Kathy had no idea. All she knew was that her body turned cold, and she shivered for nearly half an hour while her hands tingled. She tried to convince herself that it must be the air con or the weather. That could only happen so many times, though.

Now, she was worried. Now, it had interrupted an important social gathering, and Brooke had seen it. It was real. Something was happening to her, and she was terrified that it might jeopardize everything she and Brooke had been building.

"What are you feeling? How long has this been happening?" asked Brooke as Melissa exited the parking garage into the too-bright sun.

Kathy held Brooke's hands and took a deep breath, preparing herself.

"It's mostly feeling cold suddenly, and my hair has been falling out a bit more, and…well, my hands have this weird coming-back-to-life feeling, like that feeling you get when you hit your elbow, you know? It's been going on a few months, but I just thought it was nothing."

"Well, it's obviously not nothing. Did you see a doctor?" Brooke asked, trying to keep the concern from her voice.

"No. I guess I should," Kathy said, the guilt of her denial possibly making her condition worse.

"Oh, Kathy, I'm sure it's nothing serious! Yes, let's get you an appointment. Okay? You'll be fine!" Brooke said with the certainty only a younger woman could have.

"Yeah, you're right. I'm sure you're right," Kathy said aloud, both to comfort Brooke and to convince herself.

"Look, it's a beautiful day, and we suddenly have the afternoon to ourselves. Let's soak it in. Walk off the stress of everything. How about we change into sneakers and take a walk in Central Park?"

"Sure. Yes. That sounds lovely. You're right," replied Kathy.

The two friends sat silently, trying to brush off their respective fears as they made their way back to the estate.

A few minutes passed, and the car came to a stop in front of the main entrance to the gilded-age mansion. Brooke opened her curbside door quickly—hitting a cyclist's front tire with gusto in the process.

Kathy watched in horror as a man wearing a helmet and blue and white Lycra shirt toppled to the curb just beyond the bike lane, crashing hard in front of the estate.

"Oh my god, oh my god, oh my god!" Brooke shouted. Looking back, Brooke saw Kathy scooting toward the open curbside car door and added, "I can't believe it! We can't afford this! Not with everything else! We are going to go broke!" She continued squealing, "Ohmygod ohmygod, ohmygod!!!" adding only, "Sir, are you all right?" as an afterthought.

"What the fuck, lady? You have *got* to be kidding me," the cyclist said in a thick Bronx accent as he stood and shook his head while brushing off his spandex shorts.

"I'm sorry, I'm sorry. I know, I…I wasn't paying attention, and well…I'm just so sorry," Brooke replied, hoping above hope he didn't call the cops or, worse, a lawyer.

"Are you hurt? Can we help you in any way? Is your bike okay?"

Snapping his line of sight away from Brooke and down to the

sidewalk, the man remembered he had a bike and looked it over carefully, then grabbed it by the handlebars, setting it upright on its wheels.

Exasperated, he replied, "I'm alright. Looks fine…But I swear to god, I will fucking sue you if I wake up with so much as a headache tomorrow."

He hopped back onto his bike and muttered, "Some fuckin' people," and began peddling away, looking back only to add, "Pay better fucking attention next time, will ya?"

Silence descended as the two women watched the man slowly merge back into the bike lane. Kathy was relieved the incident was over and took flight toward the door, as she often did in these types of situations. Abruptly, Brooke stopped her mid-step with a firm hand on her shoulder, waiting for the man to be out of sight.

Kathy thought Brooke was behaving strangely.

10 REGRETS

The mattress in the center of the rose-wallpapered room felt uncomfortably firm to Kathy as she laid back on top of the comforter fully clothed. Her thoughts spun frantically, and she felt trapped in her body as she tried to sort through all that had happened.

Yes, the last year had been a whirlwind, but up until now, she had been doing well—she felt safe. Well, as safe as she could, considering her ex-husband and Henry were still out there somewhere.

And then the lie.

And now her health was in question.

While she knew she should have seen the doctor sooner, she was so scared of the results she had avoided it. No one symptom was monumental, she reasoned…but put together? It didn't paint a pretty picture. Her mother had died young, and she had had an unusually stressful life. They say cortisol can affect everything. Maybe that's what was happening? Her all-encompassing desire for the art collective to be a success wasn't mere vanity—it was the culmination of her entire professional career. She felt scrutinized by everyone across the street at MoMA, and now her health…this was absolutely not the time for something serious to happen.

For the next hour, she went down the internet rabbit hole, searching for her symptoms online, and instead of quelling her worry, her research left her feeling more distraught than ever.

And if all that wasn't enough to worry about—*what* was going on with Brooke? What was she talking about not being able to afford a lawsuit? Money was the least of their concerns, or so Kathy thought.

Maybe she's hiding something? Perhaps she owes terrible people money? Oh no, I should have asked for a background check! I am so stupid. I should ask her about it, but what if she reacts badly and decides we shouldn't be partners? It's me, after all, that's being accused of fraud. This is such a crucial time—what if Brooke gets mad? I've never seen her temper, but it doesn't mean it's not there. What if she bolts, disappears, and leaves me with this estate, the renovations, the entire mess, and my health scare turns out to be something serious? This can't be happening, she thought, distraught.

Exhausted and discouraged, a tear rolled down Kathy's face onto the comforter as she closed her eyes. Still, she found no tranquility. Her mind simply changed points of view from looking at the ceiling to imagining herself lying in the center of the bed, looking forlorn and ill. She hated what she saw: a victim. She let the tears flow while trying to take steadying breaths for a while. Ten minutes? Twenty? Kathy didn't know, but she felt better after letting it out.

Emotionally wrung out, Kathy swung her legs over the bed to a seated position, black slacks resting easily, her nylon-covered toes brushing the floor. *Do something, Kathleen,* she told herself, trying to move forward. *Make a plan and execute the plan; that's all you can do.* The mantra she had created with the help of her therapist came to her: *Control what you can, and the rest will fall in place.*

Kathy took her phone out of her pocket and called her doctor's office before she could change her mind.

As she added her forthcoming appointment to the calendar on her phone, she was startled by a knock on the door. Dread renewed, she asked who it was, even though she knew.

"It's me," said Brooke remorsefully. "Can I come in for a few minutes?"

"No…um, I'm just…I'm not ready to talk," replied Kathy with all the courage she could muster.

11 BUDDY

All hours of the night, huh? Let's see about that, thought Brooke recalling her mother's words as she tossed from her right side to her left in bed - something she had done for nearly two hours.

Holding her phone and hands at the ready, she paused. I could wake him… and he does have school tomorrow, she considered. She was always doing this! She scolded herself for indecision. In her work life she knew what she wanted to do and she did it. No questions asked. But when it came to family, she waffled on every decision, even something as god damn stupid as texting in the middle of the night.

Oh, fuck it. He will either respond or not. He might get mad, but oh well – he will bounce back tomorrow. Brooke concluded.

Brooke: Hey buddy, mom came here. To the mansion. She's staying here for a few days. How are you doing? Everything ok at the neighbor's house?

Somewhat relieved that she had sent the message, Brooke set her phone beside her on top of the comforter and continued inspecting the ceiling for flaws while her thoughts raced.

When had she started calling him buddy? Must have been Kindergarten. Dang, he was such a little cutie! He tried so hard to be a big boy, so she started calling him buddy. It was easy, not too far from Eddie, but she could tell he stood a little taller with pride when she called him that.

Not a minute after she had sent the text, she felt a short vibration. She grabbed her phone and saw the green message bubble notifying her that her little brother had written back

Eddie Is The Best: Hey sis. That's crazy, I had no idea she was going to see you. I thought she was with the boyfriend.

So he knows about the boyfriend? God, that kids been through a lot. I wish I was there. Maybe he could move here after high school.

Eddie Is The Best: Yeah, I'm all good, seriously. Sean's family is very chill. Kinda feels like summer vacation, but you know, with school. School sucks but whatever, I should pass with Cs.

Brooke: Yeah? Okay. Well, I sent you a birthday card. Happy birthday by the way!!! And there's some money in there. If you end up using it for something stupid like food because mom isn't around, just let me know. I'll give you more and rip mom a new one.

Eddie Is The Best: Cool. Thx.

Brooke wanted to dig. About mom, his feelings about her having a boyfriend so soon after dad, about everything really, but she hesitated.

Eddie Is The Best: K, bye.

Teenagers are so abrupt, she thought.

Brooke: Bye, love you buddy.

Eddie Is The Best: Same you weirdo.

She fell back asleep a while later with smile on her face. Eddie was ok. Maybe even better off.

12 NO MORE WAITING

Five days. It had been five awful days since Brooke hit the cyclist and said those things to Kathy, and she felt sick over it. Not only that, Kathy's health was now in question, not to mention that letter to the board. Unease was a constant in the estate now, and suspicion of each other ran rampant. Kathy was polite, as always, and Brooke had become overly kind—the partners were walking on eggshells.

Brooke considered postponing the overnight stay she had arranged with the eight guests who had agreed to provide private feedback, public reviews, and social posts, but the timeline didn't have any give. The grand opening celebration was just over a week away, and the guest list was now over 90 people, with momentum continuing to build. It turned out that celebrities, newscasters, and socialites wanted to see the renovation and what had become of Eleanor's fortune.

Usually, Brooke would press forward without bothering Kathy, as she had done for several days. Still, there were crucial decisions to be made—final touches she needed her opinion and buy-in on. The women had made a rule: if you spent over $3,000 on something, you needed to talk about it first. So far, it had been a courtesy, but now Brooke feared Kathy would ask her to make hard cuts to decorative items that would make or break the hotel. Also, if she was honest with herself, she just needed to talk to someone. And not just anyone. She needed her business partner and her to be good again. She also needed to know that her friend would be okay. She couldn't take the uncertainty another day—another minute even.

That's it, no more waiting. Brooke set down her notepad on the marble countertop and made her way to their office.

Kathy sat at her desk, typing diligently, ignoring Brooke.

She politely interrupted, "Kathy, do you have a few minutes? There's a few things I need to talk with you about." Brooke motioned to the tasteful seating area by the fireplace.

At this time of day, the charming balcony room on the far end shone filtered white light through the French doors to the seating area, making it an extremely pleasant spot—irresistible, she hoped.

"Sure thing. One moment," replied Kathy.

Brooke sat on the large, worn leather sofa and petted Tabitha, who was contentedly sleeping next to her.

"There, all set," Kathy replied, moving over to the couch.

An expert at ignoring tension, Brooke was almost convinced she had forgotten. Almost.

"Look, Kathy, first, I have to apologize. I'm really sorry I freaked out on you when I hit the cyclist with the car door. I've just been really stressed," Brooke said, looking at her hands in her lap. "And I know that's no excuse, especially because you've been having health problems and the whole board issue, and I should have talked to you, I know. I'm really sorry."

Silence filled the air as Brooke looked up into Kathy's eyes.

Kathy nodded her head from side to side and frowned. "We can talk about my health and the collective in a minute, but first—Brooke, I don't understand what's going on. Are you in some kind of trouble? Are you in with bad people? All that you said about money…is there something I don't know, because to my mind the estate is well-funded—isn't it?"

There it was; Brooke was scared to admit her inadequacy, but it was now or never.

"I don't. Well…no, I'm not in cahoots with bad people. It's just that you're turning a profit with the collective already, and…I'm burning through cash. The hotel renovation has been expensive, and there are still more costs. Also, the day I hit the cyclist, Travis had just given me a list of expenses that was a mile long. I just…I just feel like a bad partner. I don't know if I can do this. I feel like I'm not cutting it. I feel like I'm letting you down," Brooke admitted in a rush.

"Because you aren't turning a profit?" clarified Kathy.

"Yes, exactly. I've spent over 300 grand and have nothing to show for it," Brooke said, her heart beating loudly in her ears. She didn't think Kathy knew it added up to that much.

"Brooke, I realize this is my own fear coming out, but is that it? There's nothing else you're worried about? No legal problems or anything? The way you were talking, I mean, I just don't know…I questioned everything," said Kathy.

"That's all. That, and upcoming expenses to finalize the kitchen and rooms for the dry run this weekend," replied Brooke, her heart thumping rapidly.

"Oh, and how much will that be? Ten grand?"

"Around twenty, actually," Brooke replied, biting her fingernail.

"Listen to me very carefully, Brooke. $350k to fully renovate a historic mansion into a hotel and create a restaurant is very reasonable. I know you're not turning a profit yet because we planned it this way. This is the plan. Do *not* feel bad about it, okay?"

Brooke nodded, looking like a sad toddler.

"I know what we planned, but you're already in the black, and I don't know…I just feel like a bad partner. Maybe I'm not cut out for this."

Kathy saw Brooke's innocence then, and let go of her own apprehension and suspicions of ill intent.

"I'm in the black for now. This board thing should remind you that anything can happen at any time. There will be times when we're thriving and making lots of money, and there will be lean times. That's just how it goes. Try not to make it personal."

She took her partner's hand and reassured her that they were on the right track—a team.

Brooke cried in relief and, after a few moments, returned her gaze to her partner. "Look at me, I'm such an asshole. You have an actual health issue, and here I am, sobbing like a baby. What's going on with that? What did the doctor say?"

"I forced myself to make an appointment, so we'll see. I really don't know. Some days, I feel pretty normal. Other days, not so much."

"And the emergency board meeting? Did that happen yet?" Brooke asked gingerly.

"Yes, it was a quick online meeting. People asked me a bunch of questions, and my friend, the MoMA HR director, was able to join too. I think that may have put some people at ease, but only time will tell. For now, no other board members have quit, and I gave the email to Andrew. He's looking into it to see if he can track down the author."

"Okay, sounds like you did a good job with damage control."

"Yes, as much as possible."

The two women sat there, considering all that had happened, and all that was to come.

Kathy gave Brooke a firm pat on the knee and concluded, "In any case, we can do this. Together, we are unstoppable, Brooke. You have to believe that and tell me when you're worried about something, or this isn't going to work…and I swear to do the same."

The women agreed, once again feeling unified.

13 READY

Brooke groaned as she woke up again, tossing and turning. She had hardly slept, and at four a.m., she decided to get an early start. Today was the beginning of the dry run for the hotel and restaurant. Eight guests would begin arriving at eleven, stay Friday and Saturday night, and check out on Sunday. Anything and everything that could go wrong was crossing her mind.

She got up, showered, and put on her dark green pantsuit with her most comfortable heels, readying herself for whatever might come her way.

Breakfast and strong coffee were required to function, so she made her way down to the kitchen. Travis was there already with a small crew of two other chefs. Trying not to be too disruptive, Brooke stood at the side of the room, waiting to be noticed.

It didn't take long for Travis to see her. He gave her a dazzling smile and hurried right over. "It's finally here, dry run day! Aren't you excited? Feeling ready?" he asked.

"More like terrified—but you seem genuinely happy. Maybe that's because you had coffee?" Brooke said dryly.

Travis took the hint and pivoted away quickly with a jovial flourish. He plated a fresh pain au chocolat, took Brooke's favorite mug from the shelf, added a touch of whole milk, and then pressed down on the black handle of the fresh drip coffee carafe.

As Travis handed Brooke her coffee and pastry, she asked him how everything was going with the lunch, happy hour, and dinner service prep. He explained that while the food prep was on track, they were down a host, and the walk-in refrigerator was on the fritz. They had taken care of it temporarily by going out and buying ice blocks, but it wasn't a sustainable solution.

It wasn't yet five in the morning, and Brooke already had two significant problems on her hands. Ever the planner, she took out her phone and texted two men whom she had used for years to repair various appliances in her rental properties. With luck, one of them would be available today. Then she asked Travis if it was possible to pull a host from another restaurant. He considered it and told her he would make some calls to Oliver's friends, who had mentored several people like him over the years.

"I'll try, but no promises," he said, seemingly unbothered.

Brooke was astonished by how calm and charming he remained, given the circumstances. She knew he had a lot of experience opening restaurants, but the way he was acting was almost ludicrous—as if the hustle and bustle actually gave him energy. It dawned on her then that she didn't know Travis very well at all.

Next, Brooke went to check on Kathy, to see if she was awake, and talk about the game plan for the day. Entering the office, Brooke wasn't surprised to find Kathy already on her computer. She shared that she was delighted that a buyer was interested in a painting that would auction for just under a million. She explained this to Brooke as if it were any other day, until Brooke simply could not stand it anymore.

What is wrong with these people? thought the younger partner, who was stuck in a pattern of fear and reactivity.

"Kathy, Kathy. While this all sounds very exciting, do you know what day it is?"

Kathy nodded and smiled with abandon.

"I do, I do! Congratulations! I'm so proud of you! I can't wait for everyone to see all the amazing rooms you have created. Are you ready to have a great time?" Kathy had assumed Brooke needed a cheerleader, when that was the last thing she wanted or needed.

"Yes, I guess…I'm just out of sorts. Anything could go wrong at any moment. It's a nightmare. Already the walk-in is broken, and a host called out. I mean, I'm taking care of those things …but literally anything could go wrong, and it'll all be my fault." She was a ball of nerves.

"Brooke, I think you're missing the point. Today is a celebration, a huge milestone, and we're opening for a *dry run.* People are expecting bumps in the road in exchange for a free stay. It's all good. Try to be happy!"

Easier said than done, thought Brooke.

"Now, how can I help today?" asked Kathy.

With all the worry and pressure, Brooke hadn't even considered how Kathy could help her. She was at a loss. She had been so focused on the details and troubleshooting, that she forgot to consider how she could let other people be of assistance.

Making something up on the spot, she replied, "I guess if you could stay near the gallery and explain it and the art collective to people, that would be okay."

"I can do that," Kathy replied. "But Brooke," she cautioned, "you should really consider how to delegate some of what you have on your plate. It's somewhat irresponsible to be the one person holding everything together, not to mention you're clearly stressed out. I mean, what if something were to happen to you?"

Brooke hadn't thought of that.

Kathy continued, "If you can, use this dry run as an opportunity to encourage others to lead. Be a leader of leaders."

Nodding along with her sage advice, Brooke realized Kathy was absolutely right, but wondered if it was too late. Instead of admitting her insecurities to her business partner, she simply said defensively, "Yes, got it," before high-tailing it out of there.

14 GUESTS

By noon, half of the guests had checked in, and the other half had all come at the same time and had now formed a line. Twenty minutes later, the line was not moving, and guests—very important and well-connected guests—were starting to get annoyed. The new host had sought out Brooke to ask for help, leaving the reception desk completely unmanned, and guests looking bewildered. She found Brooke in the liquor stock room upstairs.

As Brooke moved down the grand staircase, she noticed the aggravated line of people and Kathy staring at art in the gallery. In a moment of brilliance, she slipped past the line, careful not to make eye contact, and asked Kathy to help. Then, together, they approached the reception desk.

Thanking the host, Brooke kindly asked her to find the bellhop to store luggage, and she staffed the desk. Apparently, the tablet had been frozen for fifteen minutes, and the host, who'd only had a ten-minute crash course this morning, had no idea what to do. Thinking fast, Brooke whispered in Kathy's ear, requesting that she give the group a history lesson on the estate while they waited.

As Kathy began speaking, Brooke fiddled with the tablet, ultimately doing a hard reboot. A drop of sweat dripped down the back of her shirt underneath her suit jacket, as she waited the three agonizing minutes it took to restart the device. Brooke breathed a silent sigh of relief as the hotel software came back to life again, and was successfully up and running. She made a mental note that they needed a second tablet for times like this. Then, since she knew each guest's name, she began checking them in seamlessly without interrupting Kathy.

"All set!" Brooke whispered under her breath triumphantly. Then, she prepared room keys for each of the guests and stepped out of the reception area, handing them out with a handshake while Kathy spoke. Glancing at her partner, she made a circle with her index finger, giving Kathy a silent signal to wrap up her history lesson.

Seamlessly picking up on Brooke's hint, Kathy elegantly concluded her speech. It was as if the two women had been married for forty years, they knew each other that well.

"Thank you, Kathy, and thank you all for coming. You are the second and final wave of people to join us here at the Beaufort Hotel and Art Collective for our dry run. I apologize for the wait, but you are all now checked in and, as a thank you for your patience, I'd like to invite you to join me for pre-dinner drinks in the speakeasy this evening at eight p.m.—your first drink is on the house, of course."

She handed each person a map of the estate, pointing out famous pieces of art and feature spaces on every floor.

The guests began murmuring excitedly, and a few even clapped. It was a big reveal. Brooke had intentionally not published anything about the speakeasy, and a famous painting had been placed on each floor. Soon after, the crowd disbursed with smiles on their faces, save a few who made themselves comfortable in the lobby.

Crisis averted, Brooke decided she needed to calm her nerves by doing something normal. Ever since she moved into the estate, she had checked the mail daily, a ritual Tabitha loved to join in on. But, given that there were so many new people in the house, Tabitha was hiding, so Brooke had to do it without her. She waved casually at the guests seated on the loveseats near the fireplace as she made her way to the mail.

Grabbing the letters, she moved upstairs to the office and began sorting through them. Once the first piece of junk mail hit the floor, Tabitha appeared, ready to attack in her typical fashion. Brooke chuckled to herself, thinking she should have known Tabitha would be hiding there in the office.

With a smile lingering on her face, one piece of mail gave her pause. She was in disbelief as she opened a letter with beautiful cursive script on the front, and an international postmark. It was from none other than Eleanor Beaufort.

Unfolding the trifold single sheet, Brooke had a pang of disappointment that no photo fell out as it had the last time she received a letter from the intrepid globe-trotting woman.

My dearest Brooke,

Andrew tells me you are planning a dry run for the hotel and restaurant, and I must say—brava! It is no small feat that you not only took on the remodel, but accomplished your goal of creating a wonderful gathering place.

Nearly every day, I am grateful to you and Kathy for my freedom and that my legacy lives on in your hearts and actions. Indeed, while I suspected you had resolve when you visited me in the hospital, I had no idea just what you were capable of. I am so proud of what you are doing, and what you will do.

All my love,
Eleanor Beaufort

PS: I had Travis stash away a bottle of superb champagne for this very occasion. Cheers, darling!

As Brooke folded the letter back up and tucked it in the envelope, she found herself weeping with happy tears. Relieved, her shoulders fell away from her ears, and true calm set in for the first time in nearly a week.

Positivity renewed, she now knew she could do this without a shadow of a doubt.

15 UNSTOPPABLE

When Kathy encouraged Brooke to delegate, this was not what she had in mind. Making her third trip up the stairs while carrying a case of wine, Kathy quieted the complaints in her head and knees, deciding to simply endure the task.

Bone-tired, she locked the storage room located at the top atrium level and glanced at her elegant black-faced wristwatch. She noticed with a start it was nearly time for their team meeting, and hurried down the revived private staff staircase to the new exit just outside the parlor-level library room.

Once she entered, she found Brooke and Travis already seated near the hearth and joined them, taking the wingback chair across from the recently reupholstered red velvet settee.

"Oh good, Kathy is here. Now we can start," said Brooke.

"Great. I need to get back soon to make sure all is set for tomorrow. How long will this take?" Travis asked impatiently.

"That depends. Why don't you start, Travis? How was the lunch and dinner service? Any major malfunctions? Anything we can learn from?" asked Brooke.

"Lunch service went okay—the bread wasn't stored properly, so it was a little stale, and one of the customers sent it back, but other than that, no issues—still, we only served four tables. Oh, and the health department stopped by," Travis dropped in casually.

"What?" exclaimed Brooke, a shocked expression on her face.

"Yeah, it was no problem. In fact, I encouraged them to stop by after the last inspection, anticipating they might do so anyway. It's far better that way," Travis explained. "It makes them trust us. And…I hoped to surprise you with this, but I want us to have an 'Excellent' rating before the grand opening. It's a big deal for restaurants."

"What a smart idea," Kathy encouraged, although Brooke still looked as if she had seen a ghost, simply replying with a skeptical, "ooohhhhkaaaayyy." She idly wondered if her partner had ever managed anyone before.

Travis proceeded to explain the ins and outs of restaurant ratings and health inspections, sharing his aspirations to get a Michelin star. Brooke looked somewhat overwhelmed, but also encouraged by the time Travis finished, and with that he hurried back to the kitchen.

Once Brooke's attention turned to Kathy, she knew it was time to tell her.

"Well, I'll start by saying things went just fine. I moved the wine as I was asked, answered a few questions about the collective, and, oh! our friend from *Architectural Digest* popped by. Do you remember Ed?"

With a sigh and shake of her head, Brooke asked for the details of the visit, and was pleased to find out that *AD* would be doing an online update of their story with new pictures of the hotel and collective. It was an incredible and unexpected media boost.

"Anything else?" Brooke asked, almost scared about Kathy's answer.

"Yes, there's something else I've been meaning to tell you. You know those weird health symptoms? Well, I finally had my appointment."

Kathy watched as Brooke leaned forward, concerned, bracing for the worst, and then she explained it all—everything she wished she had been told by her mother, or at the very least by her friends. The doctor had done a blood panel testing her hormones, and not only was she experiencing perimenopause, but her testosterone level had dropped to near zero.

Nearing age 49, Kathy had expected menopause in the near future and was on the lookout for the traditional signs: hot flashes, weight gain, and dryness. But she had never once thought about perimenopause, and in fact had never even heard of it. She informed Brooke that women can endure difficulty concentrating, chills, irregular periods, cold flashes, sleep issues, night sweats, and several other lovely symptoms for *years* before menopause. In her case, low testosterone levels had made her feel irritable and exhausted—in addition to all of the regular symptoms.

"Years? How many years!" Brooke echoed the question Kathy had asked her doctor yesterday.

"She said the average is three to four years, but could be up to *ten years.*"

"No! That's so long! I had no idea." Brooke shook her head in disbelief, sitting in silence for a moment.

Breaking the silence, Brooke made an effort to reciprocate Kathy's vulnerability to make her feel better. "When I was twelve and in middle school, I had just started my period. I was walking to lunch like normal, with two of my friends who were boys. I told them I had to go to the bathroom, and they waited just outside. As I was changing my tampon, they overhead the wrapper rustling and yelled in the bathroom, asking if I was eating candy in there. I washed my hands and came out upset, but then realized they were honestly asking if I had candy—it hadn't occurred to them what I was actually doing. It was then I realized the unfairness of it all. Little boys still get to be kids while we are dealing with hormones and trying not to leak through our pants on the playground—and all the while, they tease us about getting breasts."

She sighed. "And then there's the whole pregnancy thing, which people say is a joy but is absolutely terrible."

"Yes. Pregnancy is glamorized still, but more often than not, it's not glamorous at all. When I became pregnant with Elizabeth, I honestly thought I was getting the flu. It turned out that's what pregnancy felt like for me: vomiting daily, force-feeding myself, and doing everything I could to get by—all while working, of course. I even drove with a trash bin on the passenger seat, it was that bad."

"That's rough," Brooke uttered, "and now also there's perimenopause for up to ten years, then menopause…for how long?"

"About another ten years."

"Damn."

"Yes, that is our lot in life. All while fighting for equal pay and respect. Ironic, isn't it?" replied Kathy with a chuckle.

"It's a wonder our population isn't dying out," observed Brooke. "Men have no idea," she continued. "If they did, they would worship the ground we walk on…"

"Yes. They either have no idea…or are in denial," Kathy agreed. "Egos are a fragile thing."

Kathy and Brooke continued to talk for a while in the parlor room, relieved that Kathy's symptoms were not more serious, and proud of a dry run that had, thus far, been successful.

Then Brooke reminded Kathy that they had one last thing to attend to.

16 SPEAKEASY

Brooke and Kathy linked arms as they slowly climbed the stairs, emotionally closer than ever, but physically exhausted. Reaching the top floor, they paused on the landing, steeling themselves for social engagement and absorbing the finishing touches of the remodeled space.

The top level of the mansion had been sectioned off into several areas. To the left, the new atrium spa and rooftop access could be seen through a modern sliding glass door. It was a humid space, featuring six individual claw-foot soaking tubs surrounded by overgrown palm, bamboo, and monstera plants, plus two citrus trees that gave off a fresh, sweet smell. Two private massage rooms were tucked away on the far end, and to the right, a small heated pool extended out of the glass panels through plastic sheeting onto the rooftop deck outside—allowing both the spa and deck a stunning view of the New York City skyline. Right now, the space was empty, but Brooke hoped swimmers and rooftop guests alike would soon discover the oasis.

Brooke knocked on the dark, ornate door to the speakeasy with a final push of exhausted determination. After a moment, a small peephole opened at eye level, revealing Melissa. Recognizing her immediately, she smiled and asked, "Names?" just as she had been instructed to.

Brooke giggled as the door was opened to them, revealing a dark, cavernous space illuminated by Edison bulbs attached to simple wires that hung from the ceiling, and cleverly placed floor lighting. The ample attic space that Kathy discovered over a year ago had been completely transformed into two very different rooms—a secret room that housed and protected the art, only accessible by a discreet latch behind a book on the speakeasy's library wall, and the speakeasy itself, which Brooke and Kathy now stood in.

They joined six other people, one of whom was the young hipster bartender with a waxed mustache just below his olive nose. As their eyes adjusted, they scanned the room. Seeing all the familiar faces delighted Brooke. It felt real. All the effort it had taken to get to this point seemed worth it.

Brooke approached the bar with adoration. Of all the rooms in the house, she had dreamt, planned, and schemed about this one the most. She wanted to honor the history of the space, while still making it glamorous. After several conversations with Kathy, Brooke had decided to keep the ancient wine barrels and plank that served as a makeshift bar during prohibition. A second plank had been added, the boards sanded and epoxied to preserve the character of the wood and create a counter-like material, and the wine barrels had been cleaned and halved to create shelves, and reinforced to be load-bearing. The result was an ancient-looking bar that appeared to be held up by old, split wine barrels. A stunning sight.

The rest of the room had changed rather dramatically. The rafters remained above, but at eight feet, walls were added and stained to create a rustic finish. The walls were sparsely decorated with a few historic photos of the estate, and three plaques that Brooke had made—telling the story of the house and explaining the significance of the space. The original rafters and plain wood still lined the external wall, where the small window and original porthole remained at shoulder height, but now there was an updated pully system. Although not operating tonight, a wooden crate with four wine bottles was propped on a stool near the window as a sort of advertisement for future orders to be phoned in on the rigged rotary phones—one near the bar, another outside seven stories below.

The final wall inside the speakeasy was a floor-to-ceiling library that hid the entrance to the temperature and humidity-controlled art room. A functional metal ladder on rails allowed access to the shelves staged with books and trinkets from the prohibition era. For the first time in a long time, Brooke stopped looking for things to improve, and marveled at her work.

While admiring the old blue-and-tan Oriental rug she was

standing on, Brooke's thoughts were interrupted.

A man said, "Excuse me, miss, would you sit with me?"

Noticing his black leather dress shoes first, Brooke hesitated as she slowly looked up to see who had appeared there while she was distracted. As her head rose, she couldn't help but scan the lean, muscular build that met her eye. His quad definition was visible through his tight dress slacks, and she suspected well-defined abs were hiding below a tailored light blue button-up shirt, the cuffs rolled to reveal his forearms. His top button opened below a strong jaw, five o'clock shadow, and shockingly familiar eyes.

Travis smiled knowingly as he watched Brooke realize it was him. Genuinely surprised, she stared at the man she worked with every day but had never really looked at before. He held two vintage martini glasses filled with a dark concoction, and held one out to her.

"Um, yes…sure," replied Brooke, gathering herself and reaching out gingerly. Travis gently handed the drink to her, head cocked, a smirk on his face. Brooke took a moment's reprieve by way of a sip of her drink, a crisp and perfectly made Manhattan. Travis simply stood there and watched, waiting patiently, slightly amused.

Kathy stood quietly next to Brooke and quickly excused herself to mingle with the guests upon seeing the unusual exchange.

"Well, Travis, you certainly surprised me. I don't think I've ever seen you in anything other than your chef whites."

"I hope it's alright with you, boss. I wanted to share a toast with you. Here, let's sit." He gestured to the nearby tufted-leather barrel club chairs.

Agreeing, Brooke suddenly felt very uncomfortable standing in the center of the small space where everyone could listen in. Moving forward six paces, she sat, set her drink on the small wooden table nearest the brown wall, and made herself comfortable. She was immediately relieved—she hadn't realized how tired she was until she sat down.

"Long day?" Travis asked knowingly as he held out his glass, and Brooke picked up hers. They clinked their glasses in endearment.

"You amaze me, Brooke. I couldn't have pictured this space and all the detail you've created, let alone every room of the estate. And now the dry run seems to be going very smoothly, "

"With your help!" Brooke interjected.

"Not really. I'm only the chef. I helped you create the restaurant and food, you brought the people and the ambiance. You are incredibly talented." Moving his glass to his lips, he concluded the toast. "I'm proud to be in your circle."

Brooke audibly scoffed and shook her head, a broad smile blossoming as heat moved up her sternum and into her cheeks. She knew Travis was not the kind of guy to hand out compliments. From everything she'd seen in the kitchen, he was stern and brisk—a highly disciplined person with even higher standards. The compliment was, therefore, incredibly meaningful.

"Thank you," she replied simply and, slightly embarrassed, took a sip of her drink. Travis responded with a single nod, his warm brown eyes lingering on her reaction.

As the Ella Fitzgerald vinyl cooed about being bewitched, bothered, and bewildered, Brooke looked elsewhere, desperately trying to change the subject. "Do you like books?" she asked abruptly.

"Books?" Travis asked with a chuckle.

"Yes?" Brooke replied with the universal give-me-a-break hand gesture and shrug.

"Yes, but I rarely make time for reading these days. I have a stack waiting for me, in fact, on my nightstand."

"Oh! I love that feeling. Looking over at a stack of books and looking forward to reading them. There's nothing worse than not having a book at the ready." She paused at her own admission and asked, "What do you like to read?"

"I enjoy fantasy fiction—swords and sorcery, as well as epic fantasy, but with a lot of exceptions too. When I read, I want to be transported into a new world, and I want to understand the characters fully, you know?"

"Yes, I love that—when you get lost in the story and the people are multi-faceted and relatable. Those types of characters can be hard to find, though, especially in fantasy—some can be super-predictable."

"Depends. It's all about the quality of the writing. Take Patrick Rothfuss. He wrote *The Name of the Wind* and the whole Kingkiller Chronicle series."

"Yes!" Brooke interjected excitedly, "I read that series twice over! It was *so* good. Plus I read the novellas too," she admitted. "Amazing writing."

"Exactly. So did I," Travis said with a smile.

Travis then shared with Brooke a few other authors he went

back to time and time again—Brandon Sanderson, Raymond E. Feist, and others. Brooke listened carefully, sharing her take on each, amazed at the depth of his observations about the plots in fantasy genres and their greater intended significance.

A natural lull in the conversation came, and Brooke realized that nearly an hour had passed, and her cheeks hurt from smiling. Not wanting the conversation to end, she changed the subject.

"Did you ever read *Slaughterhouse-Five* by Kurt Vonnegut?"

Travis said he had, a long time ago, in high school. Brooke informed him that it had been banned, or challenged for a ban, at least nineteen times since it was published. Travis admitted he and his buddies joked about the sexual scenes. It was edgy for a high-schooler to read, but he was almost eighteen—old enough to enlist—and that book was the first time he had ever considered the toll of war. Brooke and Travis continued to courteously discuss the morality of banning books, as well as the drawbacks of a society fed on revisionist history.

Brooke had not had such a fascinating and thoughtful conversation in years. The time flew, and before long, she noticed Kathy was gone. Only one person and the bartender remained in the speakeasy. With considerable effort, she told Travis she needed to sleep; it had been an epically long day. A true gentleman, he walked her to her bedroom door and quickly turned down the hall, heading toward his own mini-apartment downstairs. Brooke watched him go, pleasantly surprised at all that had transpired.

He looked back only once, a Cheshire Cat grin on his face.

17 HEATED

"You were up late," said Kathy with a knowing smile as she approached Brooke's bed at nine a.m.

"What?" Brooke replied, sitting up slowly.

"Woman, it's nine in the morning," she teased, then quickly added, "Nothing's wrong, all good. I checked on the kitchen and reception and talked to the guests already. Really, don't panic, Brooke." She sat on Brooke's bed, waiting patiently.

"Oh, thank god! I can't believe I slept in. I haven't done that in years."

"That can happen when you get laid," said Kathy, delighting in a rare moment of seeing Brooke out of sorts.

"I did *not* get laid!" replied Brooke.

Kathy raised her eyebrows in a challenge.

"Really! Truly. Though I kinda wish I had," admitted Brooke. "That sounds nice, actually."

"I don't know if that's such a good idea," Kathy said.

"Oh? Why's that?"

"It's just...he's on the staff, Brooke. We pay him to do his job, not flirt with you. If you two were having a lovers' tiff, it could impact our restaurant and all facets of our business."

"I guess, but Travis seems mature. I think we just need to be careful how we communicate," replied Brooke sullenly.

"I just don't think it's a good idea, Brooke. I don't want either of you distracted."

"But don't you want me happy? I mean, I haven't met someone in a long time. If the situation were reversed, I'd want you to be happy."

The women each stood their ground.

With a sigh, Kathy changed the subject. "Look, I'm sure you will meet someone else. It will all work out. Now, let's head to the gym before I change my mind and crawl back into bed." She patted Brooke's knee under the comforter for emphasis.

Brooke rolled her eyes, groaned, and flopped back into her bed like a petulant teenager.

"Come on now," Kathy continued in an overly friendly voice, "since everything is on track here, I thought we should head to Equinox to see if our guests are using the facilities. We can check the sign-in sheet and get our own workout in too. Maybe even hit the steam room!"

"Okay, okay, fine. Get out of here. I'll be down in a minute," Brooke said, resigned, then added, "Would you grab me a croissant when you go down?"

"Sure thing," replied Kathy cheerfully as she shut the door.

As soon as she left the room, Kathy's smile dropped. She hated arguing with Brooke, even when it was cordial. But in this case, she was right to draw the line. Dating staff could only be bad news for all involved.

Croissant in hand, she watched Brooke gallop down the stairs wearing a black tank top and yoga pants, a braid swinging back and forth near her shoulders, holding a water bottle.

The ride to the gym was a short and quiet one. Kathy insisted on driving and told Brooke that she wanted Melissa to stay and keep an eye on things. In reality, Kathy was terrified someone would attempt to steal the art from the Beaufort Collection. She wasn't worried about the money, but about the loss of the priceless paintings. Some of the pieces Eleanor had amassed were extremely rare, and would usually be protected more stringently. It was not often those types of paintings were kept just on the other side of a hotel turnstile door without a boatload of cameras and trip wire.

Once inside the luxury gym, the women asked Cindy at reception if any Beaufort Hotel guests had checked in. Only one, she shared. And Kathy made a mental note later to try to figure out who it was. For now, she asked Brooke which class she wanted to do.

"Spinning, I think. I've only been to one studio, and it was a ton of fun."

They crossed the open floor to the studio, grabbing sweat towels on the way. The class started in five minutes, but most of the stationary bikes were already occupied. They were left with two seats near the front right.

As they buckled their feet into the pedal straps, a thin, peppy woman with a ponytail and a bright red sports bra went over the instructions.

"The volume is only twenty percent right now, so if you want earplugs, you can grab them over there," she said with an enthusiastic flourish.

Twenty percent! thought Kathy. *Beyoncé's "Single Ladies" was already quite loud enough.*

Deciding to go with the flow, she turned the nob near her knees as instructed and proceeded to have the best cardio workout of her life.

A hot and sweaty forty-five minutes later, Kathy was hyped by the music and utterly exhausted from the workout. After a brief cooldown, she peeled her wobbly legs off the bike and glanced at Brooke. She looked equally sweaty, but also happy.

Fun, that was fun! Kathy realized, loving the fact that she discovered a new way to get fit and have fun at the same time.

The women cleaned their bikes, and Brooke led them to the locker room. Once inside, Kathy noticed Brooke make a bee-line for her locker to check her phone.

"Everything okay?" asked Kathy.

"No issues at all," Brooke said, shaking her head in disbelief.

"Great! Let's hit the steam room then," said Kathy, handing her a large towel. The gesture was overly polite, an attempt to help clear the air from their disagreement earlier.

Once the women had stripped down to their undergarments and wrapped towels around themselves, they ventured out into the spa lounge. Men and women in various states of undress filled the sprawling space, lounging on chairs and taking dips in small pools of various temperatures. Sweaty from the spinning class, Kathy hoped to relax and ward off stiffness in the steam room, but it was packed. It made sense—it was the weekend, after all.

She briefly checked the sauna, and seeing there was much more room, she signaled Brooke over. Kathy opened the door, savoring the burst of hot air, and selected her seat across from Brooke. It was just three of them: Kathy, a man, and Brooke. After a few moments of relaxation, Kathy looked around at her surroundings. She couldn't tell if Brooke looked at peace, or sad. Her eyes were closed, and she leaned against the side of the wood paneling, creating a kind of recliner for herself.

Kathy guessed the man was in his late forties, with brown eyes and olive skin. He leaned forward over his lap, elbows resting on his knees, dark brown hair falling forward as his hands held his temples and shaded his eyes. Once she realized he could not see her, Kathy allowed her eyes to wander. He was wearing only a towel, yet his legs were confidently wide. A small tattoo was visible on his left, perfectly sculpted pec. Even hunched forward, she could tell he had a six-pack. She internally swooned and then told herself to stop staring. It just wasn't polite.

Ten minutes went by, and Kathy wondered how long she could stay in the ardent heat, and how long the man had been there already.

"Kathy?" a baritone voice asked.

Startled, she looked around to make sure they were still alone. They were. Only now the man had raised his head and was looking at her with a dazzling smile. It was Sebastian.

Brooke was the first to reply. "Oh, it's you! Mr. Aetos—Sebastian! This is our dry-run weekend, and we wanted to see if our guests liked your gym. One of them checked in with a pass this morning, and Kathy and I came to get the full experience," she explained in a rush.

"Oh really? Huh. And how are you liking it?"

"We just did a spin class," Kathy volunteered. "It was both enjoyable and completely exhausting," she said, laughing at herself.

Sebastian chuckled, gave her a knowing nod, and replied, "I'm glad you think so. It's a good class, and people typically love it or hate it." He glanced at the sand timer on the inside of the sauna and said, "Well, my time in here is up." He secured his white towel with one hand, and grabbed the door handle with the other.

"We should get going too," said Kathy, feeling dizziness set in.

They stood, followed Sebastian out toward the locker rooms, and then both women passed him as he stopped to talk to someone coming out of the cold plunge.

Once they were a safe distance away, Kathy whispered to Brooke, "That man. Wow! Did you see his body?"

"So he's a 'fuck yes' then?" asked Brooke playfully.
Kathy nodded and wagged her eyebrows.
The women couldn't help laughing.

18 TENSION

The partners returned to the estate, and the remainder of the day went smoothly, though the lingering tension from Kathy's conversation with Brooke loomed large.

Kathy had talked three of the guests into joining the art collective mailing list and had developed a relationship with a closet art collector.

The guests came and went, and the lunch and dinner services ran smoothly, if seeming somewhat overstaffed. In the evening team meeting, Travis explained to her and Brooke that the overstaffing was intentional—the dry run served as a training exercise for both the front and back of house.

After the meeting Kathy hung around, pretending to see what ingredients the kitchen had stocked, when really, she needed to have a word with Travis alone.

"This cheese is my absolute favorite," Kathy said to him after everyone had finally left.

"Ah, yes. Nothing a good camembert and craquelin can't cure."

As he reached for a plate to prepare her a snack, Kathy stilled herself for a moment, gathering courage. "Listen, there's something I've been meaning to talk to you about…" she began.

"Sure, shoot," replied Travis in a chipper tone, reaching for a butter knife to cut the soft cheese.

"I may have seen something. And it could have been nothing, so forgive me if I misread the situation. And Brooke has no idea I'm talking to you about this, so please don't tell her."

"Sure, is everything alright?" Travis asked, now concerned. He stopped, put the plate down, and looked at her.

"Yes, yes. It's just that, well, I thought I saw you flirting with Brooke. You know, in the speakeasy. Do you like her? What are your intentions?"

Travis leaned back on the counter and crossed his arms as a smile crept into his features, before he burst out laughing.

"Oh, that. Yes. Well, Brooke is amazing. I must admit I've been impressed with how she takes on everything with the house and restaurant. She's incredible to watch."

"Uh-huh. Well…" Kathy continued, unsure of how best to approach this. "While you are clearly a stand-up guy, I just don't think it's a good idea. You know, you and Brooke. She's wonderful—quite a catch. I can see why you like her, but no, it's really not a good idea to mix business and pleasure, especially since you both are living here. I mean, what if something went wrong?"

"While I take your point," Travis said, an inscrutable look on his face, "I'm not asking her to marry me or anything. I just thought we might date and see how things go. You never really know someone until you've spent quality time together."

"Yes, well, I'd rather you not. I'm not sure she's ready for a real relationship," said Kathy, bending the truth.

"Huh. Well…okay. If you're sure."

"Yes, I'm very sure. And thank you," she added, "for everything you do here at the estate. You are an amazing chef."

Kathy hoped he would take her deeper meaning. He was a chef and employee—this should not be happening if he wanted to continue working there.

She quickly turned and exited before he asked any other questions.

Determined to relax, Kathy went to her room to unwind for the night and readied herself for bed. She stared at her ceiling for a full twenty minutes before realizing she wasn't that tired, just tense.

A remedy that often worked for her was a long, hot soak in a tub. She sat up out of bed, put on her swimsuit and robe, and headed for the spa.

Approaching the glass door with trepidation, Kathy peered in to check if she would be alone. Self-conscious from years of degrading remarks from her ex-husband, she was still shy in certain circumstances, and being seen in a swimsuit was one of them.

She opened the door and took another look around. Relieved the space was indeed empty, she grabbed a towel and dipped under and through a canopy of banana and palm trees. Stepping past the last claw-foot tub in the row, she placed her towel and robe on the bamboo wall hook. The edge of each tub was fitted with a small shelf and, helping herself, Kathy added a hibiscus lavender bubble bath blend to her tub and turned on the water to her preferred temperature.

As the slightly scalding water rushed into the immaculate tub, Kathy breathed a sigh of relief and took out her hair clip, allowing her gray-brown hair to fall to her collarbone. *God, that feels good*, she thought as she stepped into the tub, the sudsy water coming to just above the ankle. Stilling herself with deep breaths, she eased herself into the tub as it continued to fill, sitting opposite the spigot and resting her head on the small cream pillow that had been secured to the edge. *Brooke really thought of everything*, she murmured to herself before closing her eyes. She focused on the sound of the water rushing into the tub, which was her only goal, and lost herself for a few minutes in that simple joy. *It's working*, she thought, utterly relieved to be rid of the lingering strain of the day.

The only thing that was bothering her was her swimsuit. Typically, when she would come here with Brooke, they would dip in the baths nude and catch up about business and everything else. Now, however, she wore her black one-piece—ill-fitting as it was—given the possibility of guests. Eyes still closed, Kathy reasoned with herself that it was very late, no one was there, and determined to relax, she kept her eyes closed as she removed her suit and placed it on the edge of the tub, careful to keep her neck and body down under the warm water and thick layer of bubbles. Not a moment later, she heard a loud flop and sat up quickly while opening her eyes to retrieve her suit from the floor.

Reaching over, she suddenly felt she wasn't alone.

Near the door stood none other than Sebastian. *Wait, what?* thought Kathy as she attempted to retrieve her suit without exposing herself to the incredibly handsome man who was looking at her. Her cheeks reddened, and not because of the temperature of the water.

"Here, allow me," Sebastian said, holding his towel draped over his left forearm as he walked toward her in European-style turquoise blue swim shorts, his muscular legs on full display.

Holly shit, he looks like a Roman statue. He could double for the

Barberini Faun, Kathy thought, not at all sure where to look or what to do with her face.

Reaching her in less than ten steps, he politely dropped to one knee to the black and white checkered tile, retrieved her swimsuit, placed it back over the side of her tub, and returned his focus to her eyes in one smooth motion. Kathy looked down quickly, avoiding the intensity of his stare, then carefully reached her hand to the edge and retrieved her swimsuit, slowly dragging it into the bath water with as little splash as possible so as not to displace the carpet of bubbles. Never in her life had she been so grateful for bubbles.

Sebastian stood up and began walking away, back toward the door, and Kathy breathed a sigh of relief, assuming he must have also come to the spa to be alone and was leaving. Not the case. Instead, he stopped a few feet away and placed his towel adjacent to another tub, leaving one between them. *Too close, still too close,* Kathy thought, but couldn't bring herself to say it out loud. Sebastian gave her an exuberant, full smile before turning on his spigot and adjusting the water temperature.

Exhaling a deep breath, Kathy closed her eyes and settled in, determined to keep her cool. But her mind raced, her ping-ponging thoughts matching her rapid heartbeat.

What's he doing?
Don't worry about him.
Keep your eyes closed and focus on yourself—this is your relaxation time.

Kathy's big breath, innnn and ouuuutttt echoed in the space.

Just think about the water. Relaxing, long and hot. NOT LONG!

Kathleen Elizabeth, did you just think about his…penis? Kathy heard her mother's voice say in her mind.

NO!
Well, maybe I did think about that. Just for a moment.
It's been a long time since I thought about that.
Can you still get aroused during peri-menopause?
*Apparently so…*thought Kathy, a small smile touching her lips.

Kathy opened her eyes on instinct, startled by a loud splashing sound nearby. Looking left, she found Sebastian mid-laugh, looking at her, his body submerged in his tub, his right hand holding his small swim trunks.

Plop! He threw them onto the floor.

"I thought it only fair," he said, dimples emerging, savoring Kathy's reaction.

Her eyes bulged, and her hand moved over her open mouth in disbelief. She stifled a giggle, then threw her head back, letting out a full-bodied laugh.

Sebastian laughed, too.

The ice was now broken, and she realized how silly she had been. She pretended to try to peer into his tub, attempting to give him a taste of his own medicine. He threw his head back and laughed with abandon, and Kathy noticed then a reflection on the water—he hadn't added bubbles. She immediately tracked her eyes back to her own tub then, attempting to be respectful.

After a few moments, Sebastian broke the silence.

"Hi, Kathy. It's lovely to see you here. Would you like to chat?" he said formally, as if the whole nudity incident hadn't just occurred.

She paused, judging his intentions, and then decided he seemed authentic—yes, a chat sounded lovely.

Unsure where to start, Kathy began by admitting she heard her mother in her head encouraging her not to look at his penis. They both laughed heartily, Kathy's eyes watering, her bath bubbles disappearing rapidly from all the jostling.

Sebastian shared stories about his mother, how he had lost her the year before to cancer, and how much he admired her tenacious outlook on life.

Kathy shared a bit about her family.

"My mother tried to be strong for us—my younger brother, my other sister, and me in the middle—but being strong was a risk in our house. My father had a temper and didn't like children. Thinking about it now, I'm not sure why they decided to have any at all. Perhaps it was just the thing you did, a societal tradition. Anyway, most of the time, my father hid in his work, and we were grateful for that."

Sebastian adjusted slightly in the tub, the sound of water sloshing, then added, "I think many fathers of people of our generation hid inside their work, not intentionally, necessarily, but the pressure to provide a perfect life for your family as the sole earner must have been intense."

"Yes, but some couples were better at handling it than others," Kathy argued kindly. Then, feeling uncharacteristically relaxed, she shared how her family dynamics came to inform her worldview.

"Maybe that was it. No…it would be too generous to let him off that easy," Kathy considered aloud, then continued, "My brother Charley was an accident—several years younger than me when he was born, and my older sister succeeded in being anywhere but home. My mother was perpetually anxiety-ridden."

"When Charley was a newborn, I was six, and I can remember him crying every morning until I decided to do something about it. Then, every morning, for god knows how long, I would get up and go to his bassinet and strain to pick him up, then walk to the kitchen. I'd set him down on blankets on the floor and make a bottle, only then making myself cereal after I had fed and changed him, all while my parents slept. I know now that I lost my childhood to parenting my younger brother—that and being a high-stakes peacekeeper whenever my older sister had to come home.

"It took me a while to realize that I was perpetually taken for granted, and now, as an adult, I often give people the runway to take me for granted. It's something I have to watch out for—to make sure I don't get trapped in the loop. But don't feel free to respond to that. I'm so relaxed I'm rambling," she concluded, slightly embarrassed.

"Sounds like a smart thing to do," responded Sebastian, and then he shared that his childhood had been very different. Happy, but also challenging.

A first-generation immigrant, his mother, Lela, had sold her very successful design and printing company and moved them from Athens to New York, and his father had to stay behind. This was just after the fall of communism in Eastern Europe. So many things were uncertain in the region, and his parents wanted to ensure Sebastian had all the opportunities and stability the US could offer, so his mom sold her company and abandoned her dream for his potential.

He recalled learning English as a teenager after arriving and the bullying that came with that. It was then, he explained, that he turned to sports and fell in love with soccer. It was the world's game, and people respected skill no matter your appearance, where you came from or your school grades.

When the conversation came to a natural break, the pair sat silently for a moment, taking everything in and reflecting.

Eventually, Sebastian asserted that he admired his mother deeply. Her love, her entrepreneurial spirit, her sacrifice. It's what made him decide to start the gym, he admitted, and then he asked Kathy about her work. His face lit up, pleasantly surprised to learn of all she had done with the art collective. It turned out they shared a love of art, and a mutual respect for strong women.

At some point, Kathy had fully relaxed in the tub, letting her bathing suit and inhibitions slip to the bottom, forgotten.

Several hours—marked by three hot water refills—went by as they talked, and eventually, they decided to call it a night. Sebastian popped up out of this bathtub first. Completely nude with his backside to her, he casually strode over to his towel, unabashed. Kathy kept her eyes down for the most part, doing her best to give him privacy. She only allowed herself one quick flick of her eyes, yet he caught her looking, and his jaw flexed in response. *He must have been staring over his shoulder the whole time*, Kathy realized.

Not bothered, he wrapped his towel around his V-shaped waist and then walked over toward her tub instead of leaving.

Kathy's heart raced. She sat wide-eyed, unsure of what would happen next, while he had donned a sinister smile. At the last minute, he pivoted away from her tub toward the bamboo-encased hook, then grabbed her towel and laid it politely over the fixture at the end of the porcelain tub nearest her feet, while holding her gaze steadily with his eyes.

Kathy felt stripped bare and gulped at the intensity of the moment. While she was still in the water, the view of her naked body was unobstructed, but the sculpture of a man refused to look. The moment he left her gaze, he snapped his head and turned toward the door—a modern gentleman.

Kathy watched him saunter toward the exit. Throwing a hand up to wave goodbye, he said casually, "Goodnight, Kathy. You were an unexpected pleasure tonight."

His strong shoulder made quick work of opening the door to the hall, leaving Kathy with a smile on her face.

19 HOT AND COLD

It's strange, Brooke thought, *it's like he's avoiding me or something.*

For the last several days, every time Brooke went looking for Travis, he either wasn't there or was about to head out on an errand. She was intrigued by their conversation in the speakeasy and wanted more of his witty talk about books, or anything really. *Let's test my theory*, she thought. She knew Travis was preparing dinner for the three of them, plus her mother, and she could smell the preparation wafting up from the English Basement into the foyer.

"Ah, there you are!" Brooke said to Travis, who had his back to her, stirring something boiling away on the stove.

He wiped his hands casually on the cloth attached to his waist and turned to her. "You found me. Are you surprised I'm here?"

"No, just the opposite. I hoped you would be. I feel like we keep missing each other."

"Do we?" Travis asked nonchalantly, turning back toward his meal preparations.

He's gone cold, thought Brooke, now self-conscious. Maybe their conversation in the speakeasy was just between friends, and she had imagined the chemistry. Or worse, maybe he felt an obligation to talk with her since she was technically his boss.

God, this sucks.

"Yeah. I mean, I've looked for you a few times to continue our discussion. I, uh, I really liked talking with you the other night," Brooke admitted in a halting fashion.

"Oh. Do you need to talk about something specific? Go over a menu or perhaps the grand opening procedures?" Travis asked innocently.

"No, no. Nothing like that. I think you've got it all handled, right?"

"Exactly. All good here," he responded tersely, quickly chopping herbs.

"Oh…okay then. I just kind of wondered…the other night, when we were talking. Did you, um," Brooke paused, uncertain whether she should ask the question so directly.

"What?" Travis interjected, unaware of her internal struggle.

"Did you, you know, feel something up there—in the speakeasy when we were talking?"

Travis set down the knife, sighed, and turned around. With a neutral expression on his face, he said to Brooke, "Yeah, I think there's a draft coming through that old window you want to use to deliver wine. Makes the space chilly."

Brooke watched, somewhat stunned, as he abruptly turned around.

Wow, just…wow. Brooke wondered how she could have read everything so wrong. It's like that night was a dream. He was warm, kind, considerate, flirtatious even—but now he's all business.

He didn't like me after all, Brooke decided, quietly leaving the space.

Kathy was working diligently on responding to emails when Brooke opened the door to their office.

Brooke slumped into her chair in a daze and logged in to her computer. After entering her password, a new message from the photographer appeared. She opened the photos of the dry run and was surprised to see he had also captured a few shots from the cocktail hour. Without hesitation, she clicked to enlarge a photo of her and Travis in deep conversation while in the leather chairs. At the time, she hadn't realized the photographer was there. Now, reflecting on what Travis had just told her, she wanted to look at the photograph objectively.

She looked carefully at their posture, both sitting, leaned in at a very enthusiastic 30-degree angle, their heads close, knees grazing. *Impossible. He was definitely flirting.* Kathy saw it too, didn't she? Isn't that why she said dating him wasn't a good idea?

"Hey, could you come here a minute and take a look at

something?" Brooke asked Kathy casually.

"Sure thing—one sec," she replied.

Brooke heard Kathy hammer out another sentence on the keyboard and then watched as she stood and moved around the desks and over to Brooke.

"Hey, so you remember the cocktail hour in the speakeasy?"

"Of course."

"Well, the photographer caught several good shots, and one in particular caught my eye. Look here," she said, pointing at the photo, "doesn't Travis look like he's flirting? I thought he was…and I think you even thought he was, but I swear to god he's been avoiding me ever since."

"Hmm, possibly," Kathy said cautiously.

Brooke continued, "And just today, I confronted him—well, more like politely questioned him, and he seemed cold. Ice cold. A complete 180. How could he have been so warm and engaging and now go cold?"

"It's probably all for the best, Brooke. Like I said, I don't think dating the staff is a good idea."

"I know that's what you said, and I've been thinking about it, I really have, but his behavior has been more than odd. I hope I didn't mess everything up already. I don't think he even likes me now," said Brooke, dismayed.

"He probably thought things through and came to the conclusion it was a bad idea. When I talked to him, he seemed set on keeping things professional."

"Wait, you talked to him? About me?" Brooke asked incredulously, her voice rising.

"Yes, of course," Kathy sighed. "Look, the success of our business and Eleanor's legacy is far more important than a fling. I wanted to make sure Travis was on the same page—and make sure he didn't bother you anymore."

"I was *not* bothered! And how dare you!" Brooke said passionately, her voice ringing out into the corridor.

"We talked about this, Brooke. I thought we were aligned. I didn't want you distracted."

"Yes, you briefly shared your opinion, but I hadn't made up my mind. Now everything is ruined with Travis. I bet he thinks he'd be fired if he was caught flirting with me! Ugh," Brooke lamented, "what a freakin' mess."

She stared daggers at Kathy while she held her gaze right back steadily—standing proudly on the moral high ground.

"And you," Brooke continued, "you are doing the exact same thing, flirting with Sebastian! While naked, no less!"

"That's different," Kathy replied.

"No, it's not. He's our business partner. An important ally for events, the gym for guests, and the key to our five-star rating."

"Nothing happened between us, Brooke."

"Yep, and nothing happened with Travis. But you went ahead anyway and scared him off. Threatened his job. Now he's cold to me. He could have been something, Kathy. I'm lonely. I haven't met someone I've been romantically interested in in *years!*" Brooke explained, now red-faced.

Kathy leaned forward toward Brooke, "But I was just…"

Brooke cut her off, "You were just butting into someone else's business. Lucky for you, I wouldn't do that to you. I actually want you to be happy."

Brooke stood up briskly out of her office chair and took two strides toward the door, before turning back toward Kathy. "Date anyone you like. And let me do the same." With that, Brooke slammed the door, punctuating the finality of her demand.

Turning into the hall, Brooke nearly collided with her mother.

"Brooke honey, I heard yelling. Are you all right?" she said while inspecting her face, and reaching her fingers to Brooke's flushed cheeks.

Brooke quickly batted her away.

"I'm fine. Minor dispute with my business partner." She turned down the hall toward her bedroom and added, "And you, Mother, should not be here. Get your things and go be with your boyfriend, or better yet go mother your teenage child. He misses you, even if he won't say it."

The woman scoffed, moving her hand to her chest and bending back dramatically as if she had been physically wounded, "You can't be serious?!" She asked, a smile still on her face.

Brooke stopped walking away to face her mother squarely. The women stood twenty feet from each other in the hall, a lifetime of animosity thickening the air between them.

"I am absolutely serious." She affirmed with audacity.

"You're distracting me. I have a to-do list the size of Texas to get done before the grand opening, and your *friendly* visit was not appreciated. Next time, ask my permission, or don't come at all."

Brooke turned on her heel as her mother remained silently stunned. Her cheeks were hot with fury, yet her body never felt so light.

20 PAYBACK
A MONTH LATER

"The Beaufort Hotel and Art Collective website went live nearly a month ago with photos from some kind of invite-only event," Henry told his girlfriend with a pang of jealousy as they walked northbound on Ninth Avenue.

"Yes. It is a beautiful space, and the rooms—my god. Exquisite," Alice said.

Of course you *would think that*, Henry seethed with quiet resentment. He was beginning to get irritated with the woman he had been dating, and living off and on with. *Perhaps she had outlived her utility*, he wondered.

"What was the contest like? You said you were a finalist, but then both Brooke and Kathy won together. When I first heard about it, I didn't think partnering up was an option," she asked, easily keeping pace with him.

I wonder how much she knows? considered Henry, looking at the spritely woman. Then he replied, "It was a wild waste of time. I didn't see their collaboration coming." Henry ran a hand through his salt and pepper hair and added, "Eleanor had even flirted with me in the parlor. I was shocked, to say the least."

"You're very handsome, Henry, you know that—I'm not surprised she flirted with you. Who wouldn't?" she said dotingly. "I'm just surprised you didn't partner with Brooke yourself."

"I'd assumed collaboration was against the rules!" he said in anger. "Eleanor had, in no uncertain terms, told us not to work together on several of the challenges."

Alice moved her chin down and pursed her lips momentarily. Henry worried she was onto him, but she sighed and breezily said, "Well, all's well that ends well."

But Henry was not letting her off that easy.

"Well, the grand opening is happening soon. I thought we would stop by and take a look around. There was one painting in particular I'd love to see again. I'm certain Eleanor would want me to have it."

"Oh darling, I bet she would. What a wonderful idea to stop by and cheer them on! I'm surprised I didn't think of it myself!" Alice said excitedly.

Perfect, she's not going to take much convincing, thought Henry, as Alice smiled giddily.

"And there's one thing I thought you might like to do. I heard a rumor that Travis and Brooke are dating. Isn't that something?" he said, knowing she would jump at the chance to dig into the scandal.

"Oh really? Tell me everything you know!" she demanded.

With all his plans falling in place, Henry proceeded to give her what very little information on the couple he'd been able to glean, before getting back to discussing the event. He recited all the knowledge he gathered from Brooke's online promotion efforts in an attempt to seem like a trusted ally.

21 PLANS

Kathy had insisted on going to the gym every weekday for the last month. That was all well and good, but Brooke was exhausted. Most nights, she slept terribly, suddenly remembering one detail or another for the grand opening. *It will all work out*, she told herself, as she adjusted the shoelaces of her runners.

Knowing Kathy had ulterior motives for going to the gym, Brooke had asked her about Sebastian several times. Each time, Kathy overwhelmingly denied any attraction, touting the benefits of regular exercise. Kathy still wouldn't admit it was reasonable to date someone you're working with. Brooke kept quiet about it, however, because she wanted Kathy to have a romantic partner—or at the very least, a fling.

That's why she had invited Sebastian to stay at the estate on the final night of the dry run. If Kathy was seeing someone, it was very reasonable that she could too. Brooke expected Kathy and Sebastian might have a pleasant conversation, but from what little Kathy shared about the atrium spa encounter, the reality was much better than anticipated. Brooke thought it was only a matter of time before Kathy would have to admit the futility of turning these guys away.

Kathy reached the final stair and set foot into the empty hotel lobby, as Brooke took a sip from her water bottle with one hand and tucked her phone in her side pocket with the other. The women exchanged casual morning greetings, locked the ornate wrought-iron door behind them, and entered the back of the car with Melissa in the driver's seat.

Kathy took the opportunity to check in with Melissa on how

the increased security measures were coming along.

"Hi Melissa, good morning! Curious, how is the double entry coming along?"

"Well, it's an unusual request to essentially have a trap door in a house, but we found a solution," explained the head of security. "The door will open from the library pull, like normal, and then you can step into a small holding room, about the size of an elevator, that we are equipping with two cameras and two keypads. One keypad to get back out through the hidden door you just entered, and a second to access the art archive. The trick has been rigging the keypad to the bookshelf door latch. Turns out we don't need to link them at all—they are two separate mechanisms."

"Sounds perfect. And what about the art hanging around the hotel?"

"We now have hidden cameras on every corridor hooked up to a live CCTV recording center. We took over a storage closet downstairs in the basement for live monitoring during events or high capacity times—that way, guests won't notice, and security can come and go from the secondary entrance."

"Hmm," Kathy responded, hesitant.

Brooke chimed in, helping Kathy so she didn't have to be the bad guy, "Sounds great, Melissa. Is that how it works in museums? Do they use cameras, or is there something more that keeps people from stealing paintings?"

Kathy shared a kind smile with Brooke, appreciating that she picked up the ball.

"Oh, there's a lot more to museum security. We are trying to watch the budget, ma'am," Melissa replied.

"I see. Could you give us a written proposal with what more you could do with the additional budget?" requested Brooke.

"Perfect! But no rush, Melissa," added Kathy.

"Well, actually," clarified Brooke, "there's somewhat of a rush. The grand opening is a week away, and we want to test all the systems two days in advance. Maybe we can talk through the options this afternoon so you don't have to go to the trouble of putting a proposal together?"

"That works for me, ladies," replied Melissa happily.

A few more minutes passed before the car pulled up to Equinox, and the women sat in content silence.

Coming up on such a significant milestone, Brooke considered everything they had been through in just a year. They had conspired together, kept each other safe, stepped into new roles, argued, cried, and laughed, growing apart and then back together even stronger. Even now, while at something of a stalemate in the relationship department, there was something special about their partnership.

The way they had each other's best interests in mind at every turn was comforting, and propelled their dreams forward.

Brooke peeled herself out of the car while complaining about the prospect of working out, too stubborn to admit to Kathy that exercise did help with stress and sleep.

After dropping their bags in the locker room, the women went straight to the side-by-side stair-stepping machines and adjusted the tempos to match. It was a good location, with a view of the pool in the distance and hard bodies straight ahead. Brooke suspected the latter was why Kathy chose the spot, and she didn't mind a bit.

"My daughter is dropping by the estate this afternoon," Kathy said, beaming with pride at the mention of her daughter.

"Oh really? It will be nice to finally meet Elizabeth. Is she stopping by for a reason? Or just in town?"

"I'm not sure. She just sent me a text. Anyhow, it will be fun for you two to meet—I've told her all about you!"

They left the gym without a Sebastian sighting, and spent the morning on their laptops in the parlor—posting, planning, inviting, and preparing for the grand opening.

22 SURPRISE!

I hate surprises, and Elizabeth texting this morning that she's stopping by this afternoon is definitely a surprise.

As Kathy watched Brooke hammer away at her keyboard, she couldn't help but be distracted. She loved her daughter, yes, but try as she might, they didn't have a close relationship.

Ever since Lizzy was a teenager, she had felt her pulling away. At the time, she figured it was just a phase, but then the slew of boyfriends and hustle of trying to establish her career took any free time she had. Or at least that's what she told her mom. In the end though, you make time for what you care about—and Kathy didn't seem to have made the shortlist.

Until now, that is.

Yes, Kathy suspected, *something unusual must be going on.*

Attempting to redirect her anxious energy, she decided to take one last look at the arrangement of the eastern gallery wall. She had curated a number of paintings, prints, and artifacts that seemed disparate at first but hopefully, upon reflection, would convey a story of opposing political viewpoints. As she rounded the banister to go to the main gallery, she heard a knock on the old front door of the estate.

Heaving the door open quickly, Kathy began, "Elizabeth, I thought you wouldn't be…" then stopped in her tracks, surprised.

"I apologize for dropping in. I was nearby and realized I had a half-hour gap between meetings, and thought I'd swing by to see how your exhibit is going," said Gregory, peering in over her shoulder and scanning the lobby.

Happy that he hadn't heard the rumors about her and was still a prospective buyer, Kathy took full advantage of his visit.

"Actually, you have perfect timing. I was going over placement, and wondered if you might have a look and tell me what you see. I want the viewer to see something in particular, but I'm not sure the arrangement conveys it."

While this was all true, she wanted him to *buy something already*. It seemed Gregory enjoyed lingering in the estate—and she suspected Brooke had something to do with that.

Locking the door behind him, Kathy motioned to the gallery while apologizing for her appearance. She wore loose jeans and a light-yellow sweater, far more informal than she would typically dress for a buyer. Gregory laughed at Kathy, returning an apology by reminding her that he'd dropped in unannounced, and took the opportunity to loosen his tie and undo the top button of his shirt.

As they walked the short distance, Kathy admitted to herself that Gregory was handsome, in a traditional way, but he was no Sebastian.

God, she needed to stop doing that.

They weren't dating, not even friends—just collaborators who happened to have had one wonderful conversation. Nothing more. *How was she supposed to put herself out there and begin dating if she kept comparing every guy she met to Sebastian?* Kathy thought as she stared at the east wall in silence with Gregory.

"It's political, no?" Gregory asked Kathy, continuing to look at the wall.

"Yes, what gave you that impression?"

"You have a Banksy print next to James Gillray's 'An Excrescence'—both flout political norms, dealing with location. But I don't get the theme of the whole wall."

"Well, it has to do…"

"Wait! Give me a little longer," Gregory interrupted. Ever the alpha, he wanted to be the one to put it together—he wanted to get it right.

"Not promotional, but still political. Historical. 'The Death of Marat' screams that. How on earth did you get a hold of that? I thought most of Jacques Louis-David's work was in Brussels, under heavy surveillance."

"This is not *the* 'Death of Marat'—it's an early version of the oil on canvas you are thinking of—there are flaws in this one, and it's on a canvas the artist painted over and reused," explained Kathy, seeing her opening. "This, and several others in the house, are for sale. I thought about auctioning them, but I want to give the grand opening visitors a first look. That is, unless a private buyer gets to something first..." Peeling her eyes from the wall, Kathy turned her posture slightly toward Gregory and looked at him, eyebrows raised expectantly.

Gregory gave Kathy an appreciative smirk, respecting the hustle.

"I'll have my curator contact you to do an assessment and then make a reasonable offer. When did you say the grand opening was?"

Kathy gave him the details and saw him out shortly after. A drop-in buyer making an offer *and* her daughter visiting?

Maybe surprises weren't such a bad thing.

23 SCOUT

Brooke and Elizabeth exchanged niceties at the marble countertop of the new restaurant, where the breakfast buffet and coffee station were to be arranged for guests. Kathy, Brooke, and Elizabeth were getting to know each other over pastries. Travis was on the other side of the bar, acting as their impromptu waiter. Behind him was a light blue tile with a steel-surrounded horizontal cut-out in the middle, a passthrough where future plated dishes would be sent by kitchen staff and picked up by runners.

Brooke let Elizabeth and her mother catch up and took the opportunity to observe Travis keenly. Though they had been nothing but cordial to each other since that night in the speakeasy, to her chagrin, she wondered if Travis still harbored feelings for her. She certainly still had feelings for him. He stood near the entry of the passthrough, organizing silverware with his hands and avoiding making eye contact with the group. She assumed that he was attempting to give them privacy. He had this effortless way about him when he was moving in the kitchen. She suspected he really did love his job. It was not often he let his guard down, breaking out of formal employee mode, but when he did, Brooke found herself spellbound.

As she studied his features, the circular glass lights above the bar emphasized his rich chestnut hair, while the gray and blue quartz countertop brought out his hazel eyes. She had it bad.

"Don't you agree, Brooke?" Elizabeth asked, which snapped her out of her daze.

"Yes," she said, having no idea what was said.

"That's what I thought—everyone had Napster. See, Mom, I

can't believe you wouldn't let me download music!" she argued, about two decades too late.

Brooke smiled, now knowing they weren't discussing anything important, simply walking down memory lane.

"I'm sure she meant well, and it is handy for me that she has a high standard of integrity. I wished I had had fewer rules, too, as a teenager, but now I can see my parents were trying to protect me. Little did they know they went a bit too far, and all I wanted to do was rebel," said Brooke.

If she had to pick sides, she would always politely defend her business partner.

As they conversed, Travis left in a rush to get everything he had planned to do done before the evening shenanigans. Kathy had insisted they all go out to scout live music, the goal being to recruit musicians to play at the grand opening.

The Bitter End had been an iconic venue to scout up-and-coming musicians since the seventies. Located in Greenwich Village next to a famous comedy club, Brooke had only been there once before, and the venue was already packed, just like it had been last time.

The red door was propped open, and an elegantly dressed gentleman checked their identification before letting them into the hall, down the stairs, and into the cozy cave-like space that held closely aligned two-tops and an exterior row of dark red leather-clad booths, all theater-style, giving each seat a view of the performers. The chalkboard adjacent to the stage listed the names and times of four ensembles that would play tonight.

The place was packed, but luckily Kathy had called ahead and reserved a table. The host shuffled them to the front and moved two tables together. Already, the music was so loud that Brooke could hardly think. Maybe it was covering up the rattle of the subway? On the bright side, she had an excuse to lean closer into Travis to test if there was still chemistry between them—and she intended to take full advantage of that.

Once settled in their seats, each person shouted their drink order to the waitress: Kathy an Aperol Spritz, Brooke an IPA beer, Elizabeth ordered a Shirley Temple, and Travis ordered the same as Brooke. *That's a good sign*, she thought—*or maybe he just likes beer?* She didn't know. The limbo of their relationship was awful. Not only was the stress of the grand opening and success of the hotel on her shoulders, she had no romantic partner to turn to. She hadn't thought that was important until the speakeasy night when their conversation had come so easily.

After the first set, Brooke realized that she was happy to be out on the town, and with Travis no less. The simple relief of leaving the estate and listening to live music seemed to take the edge off. But she needed to watch herself and keep it professional with Travis. It was easier said than done when the space was so small and the chairs so close that their knees were touching.

Kathy seemed to enjoy talking to Elizabeth and generally fawning over her, as mothers do—light touches to her hair, pats on the leg or shoulder, and the occasional attempt to hold hands. Brooke watched with longing as a violinist performed his solo, realizing for the first time that she would like kids someday. She had never before had the itch. It was always, someday, maybe. And that was normal for women of her generation. But now, she could see it, and hope for it someday.

Brooke glanced at Travis, looking at his profile in the dim light. *God, he is beautiful*, she thought, then struck up a conversation. At first, he was reluctant and appeared to be trying to listen to the band in earnest, but after a few questions, he gave in and turned toward Brooke with a smile. Lately, Travis had been all business—now, he was genuinely having a good time. And so was she.

Then, after the good part of an hour, Travis asked Brooke nonchalantly, "With so much on your plate, how do you find time to date?"

Brooke laughed and nearly spit her beer everywhere, shocked by the question. Maybe he wanted to get involved too, but Kathy's remarks had turned him away…or perhaps he was still interested. *Why else would he want to know if I'm dating anyone?* she reasoned.

"Dating. Well, my dating life is awful, nonexistent, really," she said coyly.

"Really? I'm surprised. You have a lot of flexibility in your schedule now with the estate and all."

"Yeah, but I also have a lot of responsibility—as you know, the weight of the launch is heavy on my shoulders. Like literally, knots in my shoulder blades. And my mom is still in town, stopping by and making underhand remarks, not to mention she's jealous of Eleanor. Eleanor, of all people—the woman who gave me a mansion and endowment! But anyway, I guess I *could* go on dates—it's just that last year, I had several awful experiences on dating apps and decided to take a break. I was hoping to meet someone in real life," Brooke said, testing the waters of Travis's interest.

"I get it. I tried the apps for a while, too, but I don't know…it's hard to find people who aren't superficial, and you never know what people's motives are. Also, finding someone who is good with my schedule is next to impossible, so yeah. No apps for me."

Brooke winced, feeling bad that she could be holding him back not only from them being together, but also from dating someone else.

"Don't do that—my schedule isn't your fault, Brooke. Remember, I was working for Oliver and the Beaufort Estate way before you inherited it. It's just a tough profession, a profession I chose, and love."

Visibly relieved for his perspective and pivot of the conversation, Brooke replied, "I guess that's true. I'm glad you love your work. I think I love my work, but I don't know. There's so much riding on the next few weeks. Kind of make-or-break. I think if we make it through the grand opening and get our bookings up, then I'll feel okay about it all," she said, moving her fingernail toward her mouth and then stopping once she realized her nervous habit.

Travis saw her catch herself, and they smiled knowingly.

Then, to her surprise and delight, under the table, Travis patted her left leg a couple of times and then clasped his hands back in his own lap. His hand was warm, and the gesture made her melt. Brooke looked at him for a moment, scanning his face, wanting to convey just how much she wished they could be together. She gave him a kind, closed-mouth smile.

At the very least, they were friends, good friends, she thought. *That was enough for now.*

24 SHOCK

A*ll in all, it was a successful outing*, thought Kathy, pleasantly enjoying the sway of the green line heading north. She glanced at Elizabeth beside her and linked arms with her, thinking fondly of when she was first tall enough for them to do that. It must have been middle school. Her little girl was all grown up now, and it was both wonderful and slightly terrifying to have no idea what goes on day to day with your child—even if they are a competent adult.

They stopped at Fifth Avenue and exited the subway, slowly taking the stairs to the surface. Once out on the street, the red hand of a crosswalk sign stopped them in twos—Kathy and Elizabeth, arms linked, and Travis and Brooke walking side by side behind them.

While waiting for the signal indicating it was safe to cross, suddenly Elizabeth turned and said, "Okay Mom, I can't wait a moment longer. I'm totally in love with Jerome and well, we're pregnant."

Kathy thought she had misheard and stood there stunned, waiting to be corrected.

"Sorry, what did you say?" she asked as the white ok-to-cross symbol illuminated.

Travis and Brooke went to step forward but stopped abruptly when they noticed Kathy and Elizabeth facing each other with no intention of crossing.

"Jerome and I are totally in love, and we made a baby! Aren't you excited?" Elizabeth said enthusiastically.

"Um, I want to be. But what about college?" responded Kathy honestly and with a heightened sense of awareness—she no longer saw anything around her except her daughter's face.

The next thing she knew, Brooke was pulling them backward to stand beside the nearest brick building and out from the edge of the crosswalk. The four of them now faced each other in a small group, Kathy looking frantically at Elizabeth for her answer.

"Don't worry, Mom, I plan to finish college while pregnant. I'll need to add one additional course a quarter to make it in time. I can't wait for you to meet Jerome—he's the most loveable man imaginable."

"Okay." Kathy hugged her daughter, not necessarily because she wanted to, but because she was worried she would say something wrong. She wanted to be supportive, but this situation was less than ideal.

"Let's walk the last few blocks while I process this. Okay?" she said.

"Fair," said Elizabeth, trying to stay positive.

Kathy looked at Brooke in desperation. She suddenly had no idea where they were or how to get back to the estate.

"I'll lead the way. You two enjoy each other's company," Brooke said, coming to her partner's rescue.

While they all walked in silence, Kathy's mind was racing, and her tears could not help but flow through the constant mix of emotions and a slew of worries that hit her.

My baby is having a baby! The realization was so strange, both happy and sad. It represented the loss of something that was hers. The loss of her little girl. She still remembered the sweet and stinky newborn smell she would savor by sniffing baby Elizabeth's neck.

Then it dawned on her. *This makes me a grandmother—I don't feel like a grandmother! How could I possibly be that old?* She had in her mind the idea of an old, wrinkled lady knitting or watching her shows, and she wasn't that—not at all. She felt like she had just stepped into her power, finally creating her own destiny and livelihood. Maybe she was missing the grandma gene.

Now, she tried to imagine Lizzy as a mother. She had always been a kind kid—sharing had come easily and stemmed from a genuine desire to be liked, and she wanted to stay busy. These days, she was thoughtful and still put everyone else first. Yes, she would make a great mother. The thought provided some comfort.

Then worry set in. *What will they do? How will they feed a child?* Elizabeth had a decent part-time job as a newspaper columnist, but would that be enough? Kathy knew nothing about the father of the baby and hadn't even met him yet. *Was he a kind man? How long have they been dating? Did they plan to marry?*

So. Many. Questions!

Take a breath! Calm down! she told herself. *All will be okay. It has to be, and I will make sure of it*, she vowed as she held Elizabeth's hand silently in a gesture of love and solidarity, all the way to the estate.

Determination reinvigorated Kathy as she decided her new priority was finding out if this man was good enough for her daughter, and if not, she would castrate him herself.

25 NIGHTCAP AND NIBBLE

Brooke stepped forward with her key to unlock the door to the estate. Melissa was off for the night, and they had the rare experience of coming home to an empty house.

The space felt cavernous and beautiful, but hollow all the same—missing the buzz and energy of people. Upon entering the lobby, the hall was illuminated with automatic lightbulbs in chandeliers that were installed a few months back. The effect was a vast, warm glow on everything in view, running all the way up the stairs. Instead of finding the space as comforting as she had designed it, though, Brooke found the scope of responsibility crushing and the glamorous ambiance without people very lonely.

She held the door—Kathy and Elizabeth entered, and then Travis came next.

"We're going to catch up in the parlor room," Kathy announced, with a downward you-are-not-invited glance—no doubt they were going to unpack the surprise pregnancy announcement that Elizabeth dropped just outside the subway station.

"Are you hungry?" Travis asked Brooke casually, as she watched her business partner walk away.

"Yes, starving! How did you know?" she asked.

"You get a bit…pensive when you're hungry. Your jaw clenches, plus a few other things. Besides, I'm hungry too," responded Travis.

Huh, he is paying close attention to me—that's something, thought Brooke.

As she followed Travis down the steps into his domain, she had a height advantage and was struck with the sudden desire to touch his soft, curly hair. She resisted, but just barely, deciding to grip the handrail instead.

On arriving in the English Basement, Travis didn't waste any time, and neither did Brooke.

"Hey, did you talk to Kathy about us?"

It was a question she already knew the answer to, but she wanted to hear it from him. She needed to know she hadn't imagined things.

"Well, she came to me, but yeah. I didn't go into detail but she had already suspected something," he responded.

Brooke was just glad he was telling the truth.

The kitchen in the English Basement always made Brooke feel comfortable. Something about the old fireplace and low ceilings—it felt old. It *was* old, with only new kitchen necessities purchased recently. The rest of it felt like an old English cottage, with its uneven plaster, exposed beams, warm wood tables and shelves, and four large brown high-back armchairs near a partial bar adjacent to the dining table and kitchen.

It was comfortable, and Brooke was a little drunk. Just a little. Rarely did she have more than one cocktail. Tonight, she had four beers.

Brooke took a big breath and supposed that made sense, watching casually as Travis took command in the kitchen. She debated where to sit. She was embarrassed that she hadn't told Kathy herself, and angry that she had preemptively talked to him.

And now their night out, with small advances that seemed they couldn't be helped. It was all so confusing. She wondered what Travis wanted from the relationship. Maybe he thought that *relationship* was too significant of a word. Did he want a casual fling? And it did seem unethical. Travis was technically her employee—she cut his paycheck and defined his hours. For that reason alone, she should avoid anything other than professional camaraderie.

The chairs were too comfortable—she worried she would fall asleep before the food was ready, so she decided to perch herself atop the island counter.

"Brooke, are you alright about it? I hate that I talked to Kathy without talking to you first," Travis offered.

"I just…I'm worried about how it all looks. How it is. I'm, you know, technically your employer…and I understand if you want a fling, but I don't know if I can do that. It's all new territory, and…" She looked at the floor and trailed off, at a loss for words.

"Brooke, look at me."

She lifted her head hesitantly; Travis's eyes were captivating, and she was sad she might be sabotaging something before it had begun.

"I'm glad you want to talk about this. I want to talk, too. I want more than just a fling with you. I like you, and have for a long time. It's only recently that I decided to come onto you. I was trying to wait until after the grand opening, but I couldn't help it…you're so beautiful and smart."

Brooke felt dazed. *Did he really just say that?* "For a long time? How long? Did I just not notice?"

"Well, I thought you were cute since the contest, but when we started planning the restaurant together, and I got to know you, that's when I…well, I started to like you," said Travis.

"All this time? Wow. Okay. Well, I like you too. It's just…complicated. So I'll be clear," Brooke said with resolution. "I want a relationship. I want someone I can have a future with—I'm tired of dating," she admitted, immediately worried she may have said too much.

She watched Travis move fluently throughout the space as she shimmied her backside to the counter, positioned her palms, and lifted herself up. Once settled, Tabitha, who was lying on the other end of the counter, stirred and opened her eyes only to verify it was Brooke, then immediately resumed her nap.

Ah, to be a cat, thought Brooke. No responsibilities, free room and board, endless naps, and a lifetime supply of bacon. It's no wonder Tabitha never so much as approached the front door. She had it good, and she knew it.

Watching a handsome chef cook her a late-night meal in this beautiful setting made Brooke remember that she had it good, too. She really did. Sighing with relief, she simply watched him for a few minutes in silent gratitude.

Turning toward her on the counter, he stopped abruptly, a plate in one hand, a fork in the other. Brooke watched as his pupils dilated. The air that had one moment ago been cozy and hazy was suddenly intense.

"I think we should date," Brooke said out of the blue. She was giving him the answer to the question they had both been grappling with.

She clarified, "And if either one of us wants to stop dating, we just say so and pretend it never happened. No hard feelings."

"Absolutely. No hard feelings," Travis said with thinly veiled enthusiasm. "May I feed you?" he asked as he approached the counter, sliding intimately between her legs.

Brooke could only nod. *Oh my god, is this really happening?* she wondered, bewildered.

He picked up his fork and gingerly brought it to her lips.

She opened her mouth and tasted the most amazing goat cheese omelet of her life. She closed her eyes and moaned, entirely overwhelmed by the smooth, buttery taste. When she opened her eyes, Travis was *right there*—staring at her lips. Intrigued, she looked at him, really looked at him. *So* sexy. *Too sexy.*

As if he had heard her, a quiet clink sounded as he set down the plate and fork while continuing to look at her with what she could only guess was yearning, his face just inches from hers.

Nervousness bubbled up to the surface in Brooke. "Are, aren't you…hungry?" she asked, trying to understand this beautiful man and trying desperately not to move too fast.

"I am. Definitely. Very hungry," Travis replied in a deep voice—a tone and cadence Brooke had never heard from him before—while holding her gaze.

The energy in the room was electric. Brooke was magnetized by him. She moved her chin ever so slightly toward him, and he closed the gap instantly. His hips pressed on the counter between her jean-clad thighs, his hands gently cupped the sides of her head, and her lips were on his. His kiss created an intense sensation in her gut, and all the stress she had been carrying gave way. Her heart rate spiked as she led a flood of lust-fueled, ravenous kisses, which he met and returned. They devoured each other for several minutes before coming up for air.

Travis cleared his throat, stepped back with heroic restraint, and ran a hand through his hair. "Would you like a nightcap along with our nibble?"

"Can you be the nightcap?" Brooke replied, now emboldened by their kiss, a smirk on her face. Travis responded with a mega-watt smile.

At first, they made out with the ferocity of high-school students and then, later, the languid maturity of grown-ass adults. This went on for almost an hour before Travis suggested they should get some sleep.

Although reluctant, Brooke agreed, gave Tabitha a pat, and went upstairs to her room to contemplate all that had happened.

26 CONTROL

"I have so many questions, I hardly slept," admitted Kathy first thing in the morning. She had entered her daughter's room and perched on the foot of the bed, just as she had when she was a girl.

"Give me a moment, please," Elizabeth responded, slightly irritated that her mother had come into her room uninvited. "Meet you downstairs in five?"

"Sure thing," replied Kathy with a smile on her face, reminded of how grumpy Lizzy was in the mornings.

When Elizabeth met her mother downstairs, the floodgates opened.

"How well do you know this guy? Have you done a background check? How old is he? Lizzy, he could be some creep that could use you and leave you and the baby with nothing!" Kathy said frantically.

A mother's worry for her child holds no bounds. Kathy had decided she would absolutely never let her daughter repeat the mistakes she made—trusting too soon, moving too fast.

"A background check? Do you think he's dangerous?" Elizabeth took an audible breath and then replied calmly, "Let me ask you this: if he was white, would you still be suggesting a background check? Before you answer that, really think honestly."

"I, uh, I don't know," Kathy said, exhaling. This was all too much. Her brain was starting to scramble—there were no correct answers.

"Umm, maybe? You've never told me you were pregnant before. I'm worried. You're still in college, for heaven's sake. And…I voted for Obama!" replied Kathy. "I guess I'm worried you'll make the same mistakes I did—rushing into marriage with someone you don't know well," she added, suddenly exhausted by her admission.

"Okay, but you don't even know him. All you've seen is a picture. Would you be less likely to recommend I date a black man?" asked Elizabeth.

Looking at her daughter, she didn't know what to do or how to dig herself out of the mess. "Listen, I know you consider yourself woke, but don't make this about race," she said defensively.

"If a poorly dressed white man wandered into the hotel looking lost, would you demand to know why he was here, or welcome him and encourage him to check in? What if it was a black man in the same outfit?"

Kathy kept quiet. She could see it now—her bias—but didn't want to admit it to herself, or Elizabeth. She silently pleaded with her eyes for her daughter to stop.

"Listen, Mom, I think I've made my point, okay? I know you are a good person. You are. You're just trying to protect me. This is all very fresh and visible to me because I just studied it in my psychology course, and I don't want you to be defensive. Instead, just consider that you might have thoughts about people, pre-conceived notions, or subconscious thoughts that you didn't know you had, and they can show up sometimes, and I don't want them to show up with Jerome. Okay? I *know* you are a good person."

Kathy nodded quickly in agreement, and the tears started to flow down her face.

Elizabeth continued, "But…you aren't asking the right questions, and that makes me upset. I need to know that you trust me and trust my judgment. I'm not you! I won't make the same mistakes you did. I need to know that, no matter what, you are going to support me and this baby because I love you, and I'm so scared of doing everything wrong," she said, her voice wobbling.

"You know what to do because you raised me. You were an amazing mom—despite, well, everything. So, why don't I tell you about him generally so you can get to know him, and see why I love him, okay?"

She reached out with both arms, and Kathy was deeply grateful for the hug. They pressed together, and Kathy nuzzled into her hair, holding on for dear life, mourning the loss of her baby.

Once apart, Kathy wiped her tears and squared her shoulders. "Okay, yes. Yes. Please tell me all about Jerome. Where did you meet? How did you fall in love? What does he do for a living? Are those acceptable questions?"

"Yes, I'd expect you to ask those of anyone I met," Elizabeth said with a smile.

For the next hour, Kathy learned all she could about her daughter's boyfriend. He was an amazing young man who had recently graduated, and they met in the library when he was doing research for his work for a top-tier science lab. He was an upstanding citizen, and clearly Lizzy was in love.

After getting to know them and how they fell in love, Kathy was extremely happy for her daughter. It appeared that Elizabeth had chosen a partner right, and she needed to trust her daughter's judgment.

That night, although entirely exhausted from the night before, Kathy lay awake, considering all that had happened. She had checked in a few times with Andrew, but the police had no leads regarding the author of the board letter. She feared at any moment they would receive another letter, or a further attempt to sabotage her.

Between that looming issue, her daughter's pregnancy, and perimenopause, it was quite possibly the worst night of sleep Kathy ever had.

27 LUNCH

The next day, Elizabeth and Kathy sat themselves for lunch. The restaurant was not yet open to the public, but it was finished, and it was beautiful. The dark cherrywood floors began just off the lobby where a small matching host station stood, much like a podium. The floors carried on the length of the room, ending in three large rectangular floor-to-ceiling windows with brass cross panes and arched tops. The effect was a restaurant that felt both old and new, airy and moody.

They decided on one of the six large booths that looked like a half-oval cut out of one solid block of wood that extended to the adjacent booths. They chose the one that faced the passthrough nearest the lobby, instead of others nearer to the bar and window. Kathy eased herself in, taking a seat on the moss-green pleated leather, using the brass footrail to aid her. Elizabeth followed.

Kathy's daughter was leaving in a few hours, and the Beaufort team decided to give her a special send-off meal. Travis insisted it was a perfect time to test the lunch menu.

After a few minutes, the women saw Brooke and Travis carrying food from the English Basement across the lobby into the passthrough. They watched as Brooke slowly placed each plate in the warming window, and Travis deftly placed them on his tray as a runner would.

With well-practiced form, everyone watched in fear as Travis heaved the enormous tray onto his shoulder with one hand, grabbed the stand with the other, and then casually approached the table.

After he had safely put the tray on the stand, Brooke excitedly approached and slid in beside Kathy. "You guys should have seen him. He was moving back and forth in the kitchen as if he was on skates. He was so fast, and timing himself! It was incredible to watch!"

"Was it?" Kathy replied rhetorically with a smirk. Brooke was incredibly chipper compared to her recent demeanor, and she wondered just what was happening.

"It was nothing," replied Travis, "I was just taking down the bill times of each dish. You should see me in action. Under pressure, I'm much faster," he said with a confident flourish.

Travis had acted as their personal chef for so long that sometimes Brooke forgot it was child's play for him—he was a real restauranter. She couldn't wait to see her man running the kitchen.

Then Elizabeth jumped right in, taking control of the conversation. "I'm so glad everyone is here. There's one more thing I want to talk to you about."

"Good! I have something to announce, too!" Brooke interjected.

"You have *got* to be kidding me!" Kathy said as her eyes bulged, before she bowed her head in defeat, nearly touching the table. "What on earth else could there be? Are you both trying to give me a heart attack? It had better be how good the food smells," she said pointedly at Brooke, then looked at Elizabeth, "or, oh dear, do you have food aversions?"

Elizabeth put her hand on her mother's wrist. "Oh no, nothing like that—thankfully, I have no food aversions yet. It's just that, well, Jerome and I have discussed it at length, and we would like to hold our wedding here, at the estate, in…a few weeks."

Kathy sat with her mouth agape and watched as Brooke's face took on a look of horror. Travis stilled in mid-air—a plate with a club sandwich seemed frozen in time.

The restaurant was so quiet, you could hear a fan humming in the distance.

"Hear me out…" Elizabeth continued, "I know this is sudden, and I know you aren't even open yet. But Brooke told me you want to book weddings here in the future, so I thought you could use us for all your promotional materials. You know, show people what it could be like, and like, we would get married for real—it would just be a smaller wedding. Like 200 people."

"Uhhhh, I understand what you're saying, but I don't know if we're ready for that," Kathy said. She shook her head in disbelief as her eyes watered and threatened to spill tears onto her cheeks. It was too much.

Brooke continued pitting out any logic she could think of to deny the request, "And there are many costs involved in hosting a wedding for 200. I mean, that's why venues charge a boatload. I know you're Kathy's daughter, but we couldn't do it for free—we would lose money, and the budget is already out of control from the remodel," she said, looking to Kathy to gauge if she felt the same.

Kathy nodded in support, but also in silent disbelief. She wondered why Elizabeth hadn't told her yesterday when they were alone.

"Uhh, sorry to interrupt, but the food is getting cold. Can we begin eating so everyone can taste it while it's fresh?" interjected Travis as he sat in the remaining seat in the booth next to Elizabeth. "Besides, everyone makes better decisions when they aren't hungry."

The women acquiesced and proceeded to take portions from each serving plate, family style.

Brooke sat stunned, the announcement she had planned to share now taking a backseat.

After taking a few bites of an exquisite Wagyu cheeseburger, Kathy admitted to the group that Travis was absolutely right and gushed about his cooking. Elizabeth, meanwhile, was wolfing down fries like her life depended on it.

After a few minutes of eating, Elizabeth continued, "We would pay for all the major costs. Jerome's family is very supportive, and they have given us a budget. Nothing outrageous, but I think it would cover the food costs, flowers, and outfits. What we really need is a centrally located venue with a few rooms for out-of-town guests to stay. His family is in upstate New York, just a train ride away."

Maybe they're well-off, thought Kathy. That certainly would make her feel better about the situation. But why the rush?

"When do you want to get married?" asked Kathy.

"As soon as possible. Not everyone knows we're pregnant, and we want to have the wedding before I start to show."

"How far along are you now?" asked Brooke.

"Fourteen weeks, so before twenty weeks would be ideal."

"So six weeks from now at the latest?" questioned Brooke. "The grand opening is in two weeks, so that would only leave us barley any time to plan and get everything together…not to mention accommodating the overnight guests. I'd have to check what reservations we already have on the books," she said, shaking her head.

"So you'll do it! *Thank you*, thank you, thank you!" Elizabeth turned to Brooke, jostling and aggressively hugging her.

"Nooooo!" Brooke let loose a guttural moan, one that was way too loud for the space. Everyone stopped and looked at her, as the tears began to flow down her face.

"I don't think you understand what you're asking," Brooke whispered, her voice now thick with emotion. "Weddings will be a huge revenue stream for the hotel and restaurant. For the first one, we have to do it right. No rushing, no shortcuts. And the grand opening is barely a week away! A *week*! All my energy is focused on that, and I'm already drowning…just let me think about it. Think about how we might make it work, but no promises," Brooke explained.

Kathy sat quietly, trying not to hyperventilate.

"Hear me out," added Elizabeth, and Kathy gave her a questioning glance, urging her daughter to leave it be. "I know it's too soon, but I was thinking that if you have photographs and a testimonial on the website, you could book more weddings—and not sometime in the future, right away."

"But there are some big hurdles to overcome," Brooke explained. "For starters, the food cost for 200 people. Even if we didn't pull a profit, it could be over your budget."

Making her way to the edge of the booth, Brooke stood up briskly. "And there's one other thing everyone should know. Travis and I are an item, and we're thrilled about it. We're not welcoming outside opinions at this time," said Brooke dryly, her words not quite matching the look on her face.

Turning to Travis, she added, "I'll take that drink now."

He smiled, grabbed her hand, and led Brooke down to his lair.

That night, she didn't go back to her room.

28 THE TALK

Brooke woke up to the most lovely distraction—a five o'clock shadow gently nuzzling her shoulder. A kind, sexy man was spooning her and whispering sweet nothings, but even that couldn't distract from her worries. She needed to get on with it. She reached for her phone on Travis's side table to send a text message.

Brooke: We need to talk.

Kathy: Agree. Lobby in 15?

Brooke: 20, please. See you soon.

Brooke rolled over into Travis and sighed.

"I'm meeting with Kathy in twenty. It's going to be a hard conversation. I feel for her, I really do. The letter, her daughter getting pregnant and wanting to get married here, not to mention her health issues compounding things. But I need to stand up to her about this." She gestured between them. "About us. I'm not giving this up."

"Just be civil, and it'll be fine. You forget she's a very reasonable person. You and Kathy are normally in sync, and you just need to get back to that. It'll be fine," Travis said reassuringly.

"But what if it isn't? What if I just make it worse? We're just about to launch, and I'm already drowning. It's only going to get more stressful. More complicated," worried Brooke aloud.

"You don't know that. One step at a time. Talk to her. Be nice. Now get going!" he emphasized with a nudge.

"Yes, chef! I'm going, chef," she cooed, calling him by his preferred title.

She went to her room and dressed quickly, preparing for the day and a life-changing conversation. She made her way quickly down the stairs.

"Ah, there you are," Kathy said, already seated.

"Yep, thanks for the extra five. I thought I should at least brush my teeth," Brooke said while raising her eyebrows, alluding to the previous night's escapades with Travis.

"Yes, well, about that…" Kathy began as she studied Brooke.

"It's hypocritical," Brooke cut in, defending herself. "Here you are dragging me to the gym nearly every day, pretending it's not because of Sebastian, but we both know it is. Yet you tell me not to date Travis," she said quickly, attempting not to lose her nerve.

"I can see your perspective…" admitted Kathy with an open hand gesture and added, "Is there anything else on your mind?"

"Well, that and…everything!" Brooke shrieked, continuing in rapid fire, "The grand opening is just a few days away, and my mom is *still* in town wanting me to meet up with her and tell her everything about the preparations—a distraction I don't need when I should be spending time *on* the preparations. And then there's your daughter's visit…she's lovely, of course, but now she's asking me to plan a wedding! Not to mention your health issues—I don't even know how you're doing! I'm such a jerk for not asking. Also, there's that accusation that made the board members quit…I want to believe you, I do. It's just that if even the idea that you stole got out, it would be majorly bad press, and sure to ruin everything—the hotel, the restaurant, the collective. Everything. Our dreams and everything we've worked for, down the drain."

There it was.

Make or break.

Brooke slumped back. She felt like an empty shell of herself, having let out all the anxious thoughts that had been stewing inside her. Now that she had said it all, she worried their partnership would be over. Kathy wouldn't want to do business with her anymore. She would abandon her, leaving her to bear all the responsibilities, utterly alone—something she knew she couldn't do.

Kathy looked at Brooke with sadness as they sat with what had been said. It was heavy and uncertain, the worst combination.

Finally, after what Brooke felt like was an eternity, Kathy responded. "Brooke…that's a lot."

Brooke nodded in agreement.

Kathy continued, "And I know you're used to being responsible for everything, but you don't have to be. We are partners—let me carry more of this."

Brooke was both shocked and relieved. She nodded rapidly in agreement, appreciating that Kathy acknowledged the weight of it all, but also offered to help again. This was one of Brooke's recurrent flaws—trying to carry it all. Kathy saw it, and offered to help. She didn't run away.

For the first time in a long time, Brooke felt hopeful, yet still sat in silence, unsure what to say.

"And…I owe you an apology," Kathy admitted with sincerity. "Several, actually." She paused, letting the words sink in.

Brooke gave a kind smile.

"You were right about Travis. I *was* being overbearing. And you know I want you to be happy. Although it could impact our business if you guys didn't work out, we would deal with that if it happened. We would deal with it together."

A hot tear ran down Brooke's cheek, the ice between them melting.

The older woman continued, "And, yes—I hadn't really admitted it to myself, but you're right about Sebastian. If he were interested, I wouldn't want to say no."

"Oh man, I'm so glad you can see that," replied Brooke. "I feel like Travis is the one thing that reduced my stress, and since the speakeasy night, I've been denying myself."

Taking an audible breath, Kathy stilled herself and said, "And about Lizzy, I should have stepped in when she brought up the wedding. I should have told her not to press ahead, and that you and I needed to discuss it before we agreed to anything. Instead, I let her pressure you into something you're not comfortable with. I regret not doing that."

Brooke couldn't believe what she was hearing.

"Yeah, that was a whopper—I thought if I said no, you would be upset, but I couldn't just say yes," she admitted with a shake of her head, letting her guard down again to her friend.

"I'm sorry," Kathy concluded.

"I'm sorry too," Brooke began. "I wish I had come to you sooner about everything—it was just too hard."

"Well, we're here now, aren't we?" Kathy said, laying her palm on Brooke's knee.

Brooke placed her hands atop Kathy's.

"Well, what about the board thing? And do you really think we should do the wedding?" asked Brooke.

"Andrew's looking into it to see if they can track down who sent the email, before sending a formal response…but no luck so far. After so much worry, I've decided that lies are just that—lies. People will say things about us that aren't true, now that we're making a name for ourselves."

"Glad to hear it," said Brooke.

"And about the wedding—as much as I love my daughter, I only want to do it if you think we can pull it off. If it's too much, then it's too much. That's it. We shouldn't suffer because Lizzy is being rash."

"You mean that?" Brooke was surprised Kathy was prioritizing the health of their business over her daughter's wishes. "Well, I was talking to Travis about it, and he had a great suggestion. We could hire wedding planners and event people to do all the heavy lifting. It would be expensive…but we could do it if we threw money at the problem."

"Yes, absolutely. I know you worry about money, Brooke, but I promise you we have plenty. And the first wedding we book will recoup all of it and then some," assured Kathy.

"So we're doing it then, I guess?" Brooke confirmed.

"Yes, let's. Everything for the art collective is ready to go, so let me line up wedding consultants and vendors to help us, so you can focus on the grand opening."

"Okay. Yes! That sounds perfect," said Brooke enthusiastically.

Brooke jumped up, and Kathy followed her lead. The women hugged, and Brooke let go of all the animosity she had been holding, shedding big, ugly tears while they held each other.

They were a team once more.

29 TOMORROW

It was only nine in the morning, but Kathy had already heard either herself or Brooke muttering about the date half a dozen times. Tabitha was zipping around the hotel like a kitten, feeding off their frantic energy and making it nearly impossible for Kathy to concentrate.

She decided she would need to stop precariously balancing on an office chair and get the step ladder in order to hang a very large Kelly Reemtsen painting. She loved "The Set Up" and had spotted it in the attic that first day she started taking inventory during the contest, but was yet to hang it. The very large oil on canvas depicted a woman from the knees down wearing sparkling platform heels, hot pink socks, and a bright yellow A-line dress that fell just below the knee. It was all very fifties housewife, except that she was holding a pink-handled sledgehammer. A portrait of a beautiful, feisty, and potentially dangerous woman was the perfect centerpiece for her political collection.

No one would forget this was a woman-owned business, that's for sure, thought Kathy, proud of the scandal the completed collection might cause.

Although the small bubble floating in yellow on the level indicated it was straight, it didn't look it, so Kathy proceeded to adjust it for several minutes.

"Do you need help with that?" a loud, masculine voice said, startling her.

After recovering from nearly falling off the ladder, she looked to see Sebastian in turquoise blue shorts, white runners, and a simple, yet very flattering, white t-shirt.

"No, no…well, would you come look at it? Please tell me if you think it's crooked. I suspect the estate isn't completely level, let alone the painting."

Sebastian happily helped, and the two of them adjusted the painting and stepped back and forth a few times. Then he stepped back and took in the entire wall.

"Do you follow politics, then?" he asked.

"Somewhat," Kathy admitted with regret. "I wish I read more, but there's so much happening so fast, I just can't keep up."

"Then why do a political collection for the opening?" he asked.

Another good question, she thought.

"I suppose I try to be apolitical and focus on the issues, and wish other people would too. What I'm trying to show here is that there are many truisms, many points of view based on historical events that are correct and valid, even if they are opposing. I think the tension created by seeing pieces with opposing viewpoints together could be explosive."

"You are a very intriguing woman, Kathy," Sebastian said with sincerity.

Kathy felt her cheeks flush and bowed her head. Not sure how to best take the compliment, she finally settled on a simple "Thank you."

"And what about this sledgehammer woman? What do you see here?" he asked.

"It reminds me of, well…in 1981, I was ten years old. I know, I know, I'm much older than you."

"You're only *two* years older than me," Sebastian interjected with a knowing smile. His fit physique and well-groomed appearance hid his age very well. "But go on…" he encouraged.

"Well, in '81, Sandra Day O'Connor became the first female justice of the U.S. Supreme Court, and I remember watching the news announcement on our old rabbit-ear television. This painting reminds me of the power women have, and their potential to bring it everywhere, including the highest court of law."

Just then, Brooke approached them, pleasantly surprised to see the gym manager. Kathy asked him to join them at the grand opening, something she had wanted to do before but hadn't gotten up the courage to ask. She liked him, sure, but had originally thought he was way too far out of her league. Now that she knew better, she really hoped he could make it.

Sebastian confirmed he would be there and then made his exit, leaving Kathy in an unexpectedly joyful mood. It was short-lived, however, when Brooke brought forward an unexpected thought.

"Do you ever wonder what Henry is doing these days?"

"Not really," Kathy responded automatically.

"It's just that—our lives have changed so dramatically. We're fully focused on what's happening here, and he, well, isn't. This could have been him."

"That's a dark thought, Brooke. Eleanor made the right choice, and you know it. We can't feel bad for him—he's been given plenty of opportunities we haven't."

Brooke knew what she meant—things were often all too easy for white men, including job opportunities and salaries.

"Yeah, he would have landed on his feet. He was nearly retired anyway," Brooke reasoned, trying to shed the residual guilt she felt for him.

Forcing herself to focus, Brooke proceeded to run Kathy through the full schedule for the opening, presenting a spreadsheet with rows in fifteen-minute increments, and then lamented about her extra-long to-do list.

Kathy gave her words of encouragement, then got back to her own to-do list in preparation for the big day tomorrow.

30 TOUSLED

Brooke woke up before her alarm again at five in the morning, unable to go back to sleep. She sat up in bed and leaned against the gray velvet headboard, then propped her laptop on top of her textured white bedspread. She ticked off a few things on her to-do list, and then she heard a soft knock on her bedroom door.

"Come in," she announced, assuming it was Kathy.

"Good morning, beautiful," said Travis, startling her—she whipped her head up from her laptop, shut it, and fussed with her hair for a moment.

"Don't come any closer, I haven't even brushed my teeth!" Brooke said in horror.

Travis smirked and approached anyway, placed a small wooden tray with coffee and a croissant on her side table, and then proceeded to sit down right next to her on top of the covers.

Brooke wondered if she was even wearing pants!? The nerve!!

He began lightly laughing at her.

"Lovely, all I can smell is coffee and pastry—also, you look stunning all…tousled," Travis replied, waggling his eyebrows suggestively.

"Stop!" Brooke replied as she reached for the coffee, coy and giddy at the same time.

"Well, if you want me to leave…" Travis teased, knowingly.

"No, no, don't go! I just…let me take a sip of coffee." She did so. "There, better. Now, is there a problem I should know about, or did you just barge in here to see a half-naked woman?"

Travis giggled and replied, "No problem, and the fact that you are half-naked is a big bonus. I came to make sure you ate something, and also to help you relax."

"Ugh, you're too nice. How should I relax?"

"Trust me?"

"Okay?" said Brooke reluctantly.

He instructed her to stay in bed and lie face down. While she waited in anticipation, he took his time as he removed his shoes. The next thing she knew, he was working his knees up from the foot of the bed and stopped while straddling her blanket-covered bottom. Then he rubbed his hands together for a few seconds, before laying them on her upper shoulders, which were barely covered by a spaghetti-strapped tank top.

For a long while, he proceeded to give her a fantastic back massage, but she couldn't concentrate. Her mind wandered from thoughts of guilt that came from dating her employee, to worries about the grand opening, to sex. It was mental whiplash, and it was exhausting.

"I've been rubbing for nearly a half hour, yet you're still tense. What's on your mind, B?" B was a special nickname he had decided to call her, and she didn't hate it—not at all.

"I know I should be focused on the opening, but I can't stop thinking about Elizabeth's request for her wedding here. It would be amazing. The photographs…oh my god, it could be spectacular fodder for the website, and I could also create a pitch deck to approach the art elite with."

"So what's the problem?" Travis asked nonchalantly.

"You know the problem!" she replied, frustrated. "I have zero time to give. And it would be covered in the media, like Page Six covered. If we got it wrong, it would be over before it started—it could end us," Brooke said in anguish.

"Well, you're right about one thing. *You* have zero time. *You* should not be working on that. Hire someone! Hire five people if you need to."

Brooke stopped talking or moving for a moment, then responded, "Oh…I guess we could do that. I…just never considered that I had the money to do that. I've always been self-funded and had no spare cash. I could! I mean, it has to be *perfect*. I don't know even who I would hire," Brooke admitted.

"Now *that's* a problem you can solve. There are a ton of event planners here in the city. Maybe Eleanor even has a favorite she could call in a favor to?" he suggested.

Brooke flipped onto her front, moving her hands to her breasts to cover them, "You. Are. Brilliant. Now come here so I can kiss you."

He obliged.

After an amazing make-out session, Travis stood up from the bed, straightened his chef whites, and retreated into the hall.

Upon hearing the click of her door, Brooke looked left to right in her room, wondering if she had unpacked her vibrator or if it was still in storage. Soon, she realized she really didn't have time anyway. Travis was right—she had a busy day, and now she knew how to go about doing the wedding.

Reinvigorated, she got ready, dressing in a bright red pantsuit with a white top underneath, her armor for the day.

Once downstairs, Brooke went over her to-do list again and dealt with the first items—she unlocked the glass and metal-encased revolving door, turned on the new lightbox blade sign with the custom logo she designed, and then ensured Melissa was in position, and the hosts and restaurant staff were ready.

Then, she waited. She walked around aimlessly, expecting something to go wrong at any moment for nearly a half hour. Nothing did. Then she took her laptop to a chair in the lobby with a fresh cup of coffee, and waited while distracting herself with social media.

Frustrated and relieved, absolutely nothing happened until the photographer Brooke had hired arrived. She then rounded up everyone to take photos, which took much less time than she'd allotted on her spreadsheet.

An hour before the grand opening, Brooke felt ready—everything was going to plan, but still, she couldn't help but feel anxious.

Right on time, Melissa welcomed two more team members and positioned one in the camera room, another on the fifth-floor balcony landing with a line of sight to both the ballroom entry where the main festivities would be, plus a third person down in the lobby.

At five o'clock sharp, people began to arrive for the grand opening celebration. The *oohs* and *ahs* of people from the exclusive guest list marveling at her renovations and decoration began to soothe Brooke's nerves.

All is going to be okay, she told herself, and for the first time all day, she believed it.

31 GRAND

"It's time, are you ready?" Henry asked his girlfriend as they strode toward the Beaufort Hotel and Art Collective in lockstep.

As the new black and white blade sign came into view, Alice assured him that, yes, she was ready to play her part. But Henry couldn't help but worry—he had never in his life imagined he would do something so illegal, and with someone with such competing interests. Involving Alice was a considerable risk, but it had already been worth it—he knew more information than anyone realized and couldn't wait for the look on Brooke and Kathy's faces when they found out the truth.

These women didn't deserve the estate or the paintings within. Henry had worked hard his whole life, and because of them, he had next to nothing to show for it. What business did they have owning this estate? None whatsoever. And what business did they have hiding hundreds of millions of dollars' worth of art in that shoddy old attic? Zilch, zip, zero.

Henry and Alice met Maddox Frankfort at the original door as planned, and he escorted them in while exchanging niceties. With Maddox's simple wave, the group politely avoided the stern woman near the new revolving door who wielded a guest list like a weapon. Henry had led the art collective board member to believe that he was an old friend of Kathy's, and upon telling him a lengthy history of the house, he had a brilliant idea. Maddox asked Henry if he would give a brief history of the house from the stage during the grand opening.

Henry agreed, but on one condition—it would absolutely need to be a surprise. Brooke and Kathy would be delighted, he had assured him, but they couldn't know. That's when they decided he would personally welcome him at the old entrance.

"It looks stunning! Don't you think?" Alice asked Henry excitedly as they made their way into the center of the room, which was already bustling with people.

He nodded and admitted quietly that, yes, the renovations were incredible. The marble floors had been stripped, and the wood floors buffed, returning them to their former glory, covered only occasionally with green-grey rugs in various areas. Three new chandeliers emphasized the vastness of the space, and a seating area had been created with a giant sage-green velvet couch and two wingback-worn leather chairs adjacent to the fireplace and very near the foot of the primary staircase. In the distance, past the prominent dark wood reception desk topped with bright marble, the hallway had been opened, and a gallery space glowed bright white. In the distance to the far right, the wood floor transitioned into penny tile, and a restaurant seemed to have been created out of thin air. *Perhaps they removed some storage areas?* he wondered in awe.

Yes, it was stunning. Even he could not refute that.

Alice admired the estate beside him, taken back by its magnitude as a formal tailcoat-adorned server approached with glasses of champagne atop an antique brass tray. The women had truly gone all out. As guests entered through the glass turnstile door, their senses were greeted by fresh hanging white lilac and ivy affixed to the entry. Once they stepped inside, a row of topiary—three green balls with delicate white flowers—rose from ornate brass vases and led them to the reception desk. The seating area to their left was adorned with table vases filled with bouquets of white roses and dark ivy. The fireplace mantlepiece was chock full of white candles in all sizes. Beside the seating area began the double staircase that framed the cavernous hotel lobby. The staircase's recently refinished wood railing was dressed with abundant hanging wisteria, which slowly curved all the way up the primary staircase, leveled off at the barely visible sixth-floor landing, and then came down the secondary stair on the opposite side of the lobby, creating a showstopping spectacle.

The couple walked in silent awe over to the topiary walkway. Once they reached the reception desk, they were greeted with more rose bouquets, and a stylized 5x7 map of the estate's updated footprint was provided. The map had with a key directing guests to featured areas and paintings.

Perfect! thought Henry, looking at the map with sinister delight, then he dismissed Maddox with a polite word of thanks, assuring him he knew where he was going.

Once Maddox was gone, Alice gave Henry a short wave goodbye and approached the kitchen. Henry was glad she was taking her part seriously, and watched until she found her mark. The older woman gave Travis a hug before her grilling, determined to understand just what he saw in Brooke.

Convinced his girlfriend had adequately distracted the chef, Henry made his way up to the grand ballroom, where the main event had started about thirty minutes prior. He had thought it best they sneak in late, and it appeared to be working—Brooke and Kathy were nowhere in sight.

Henry climbed the stairs quickly but slowed as he approached the ballroom. He aimed to look inconspicuous and graciously accepted a glass of champagne from a waiter who stood at the sidelines. As he entered, he kept close to the wall, keeping his back to the center, and greeted and toasted random people as he made his way around the perimeter. He knew he looked somewhat generic, and he was banking on it—wanting the element of surprise on his side.

A stage had been erected at the far end of the ballroom, and small high tables had been spaced throughout the dance floor with white linens and the same elaborate white rose and ivy bouquets from the lobby. In the center of the room, overlarge candelabras held circular floral arrangements with white flowers and green leaves, accompanied by stands with framed photographs of the estate throughout history and the Beaufort family, with small plaques explaining the significance of each.

All very elegant, Henry admitted. He had assumed Brooke's taste would have been more flamboyant—*perhaps she had hired help*, he thought as he continued to walk.

Finally to the front, Henry moved his foot to the first of four steps onto the stage, just eight feet or so from the microphone, when all of a sudden, Kathy appeared from out of nowhere.

He was startled and looked behind her. She must have been standing beside the floor-to-ceiling white curtains. How long had she watched him, he wondered. No matter. This was it, his moment.

"Hi Henry, so good to see you. How did you hear about the grand opening?" Kathy said, her disdain only apparent to those in close proximity who may or may not have been paying attention.

"There's been quite a buzz around the event, and I thought I'd see it for myself. Surprise!" he said with genuine happiness as he watched Brooke approach from the same backstage area Kathy had.

"Hello, Brooke. Good to see you," said Henry far too cordially.

Brooke looked at Kathy to confirm she wasn't imagining things. Kathy shook her head in apparent dismay. All three of the former competitors for the estate stood on the balls of their feet, each keenly aware that just an arm's length away was the microphone, when all of a sudden, a sanguine matriarch approached.

"Honey! Oh, the decorations turned out just incredible, truly!" said Alice.

"Mom? What are you doing here? I thought I was clear—I need to concentrate. I can't have you here," said Brooke, utterly confused and dismayed.

"Oh, well, I was invited, dear. While you, my own daughter, did not invite me, someone else did," she responded with an air of superiority. "This is Henry, my boyfriend—I've told him all about you. It's so wonderful that you're all in touch still. When he asked me to join him today, I was so excited! I couldn't wait to see all your hard work come together!" Brooke's mother said with a theatrical flourish, enjoying the fact that she got her way in the end.

Brooke whisper-screamed, "What the actual *fuck*? Are you two…together? *This* is your boyfriend?" She looked at Henry with ferocity, suspecting he had planned it all. She knew her mom was naïve, and since her father passed away, there was no one to counsel her out of bad decisions.

Henry was elated with Brooke's reaction. He had imagined it so many times, but this was even better.

Kathy moved forward an inch, and at the same time, Henry could have sworn he saw something flash in her hand. He looked and saw her holding something black—a pen, maybe?

Staying on task, he continued, "Not so fast, Kathy. I wonder if everyone here has heard about your past crimes? Your board of directors were certainly interested. I think this group of distinguished guests should know you are running a sham, selling fake paintings," he said triumphantly.

"You! It was you! Unbelievable…" Kathy began to say as a man in a black suit approached her side. She adjusted her posture and continued, "You would love that, wouldn't you? To grab the mic and spread lies. To ruin us. So why haven't you already? Why are you here, Henry? Spit it out," she said as Brooke, her mother, and the man in a black suit listened intently.

"Ah, that's the right question," Henry said condescendingly, "unless you want your little hotel and art collective to fail before it even gets started, then I suggest you walk me down to your gallery space, and we pick out the highest-value painting. We shake hands. Then you let me walk out with it."

He couldn't help but smile as Kathy and the suited man looked at each other, trying to convey some unspoken message.

"Henry, you can add revisionist historian and blackmail artist to your résumé. You really are a despicable person." With that, Kathy motioned to the man beside her and to Henry's surprise, he produced handcuffs, holding them covertly near his belt so as not to scare the large crowd of people who were socializing in the ballroom.

"What are you doing? This is my boyfriend," Alice said in desperation and ignorance.

"No, Mom. We have a no-contact order against this man—he's extremely dangerous. I think he was posing as your boyfriend to get close to us," clarified Brooke. She scoffed.

Kathy calmly continued, "You're not as sly as you think, Henry. I watched you approach the stage. Your advances during the contest were absurd. You tell a not-for-profit board lies about me, and now you stoop to this? You date Brooke's mother for presumably months so that you can blackmail us? Do you have no conscience!? No perception of right and wrong? Frankly, I'm not at all surprised your wife cheated on you. Maybe it's time to take some personal accountability."

Who did this woman think she was? Henry thought.

He began to move toward Kathy to give her a piece of his mind, when a large hand thumped him on his chest, bumping him back a few inches. *Right, the handcuff guy*, he remembered, and finding himself out of breath, he began to wonder what—if anything—they could actually do to him. He knew people. He had powerful friends.

"Now, Henry, here's what's going to happen," Kathy said sternly. "Sven here is going to escort you to the lobby and watch as you see yourself out. Any wrong moves or attempts to disrupt the event, and you will be cuffed, placed in a holding cell, and the police called."

"Holding cell?" he huffed. "Don't be so dramatic. I've done nothing wrong." He shrugged, feigning nonchalance.

"Is your memory going? You are trespassing right now. You signed an agreement to keep your distance from the estate and us. Your lawyer has a copy of it."

Kathy rolled her eyes, and damn if Henry didn't want to slap the smirk right off her face.

She added, "Now, be a good boy and leave." With that, she set her security guard into action. "Sven?"

The man gripped Henry's elbow tightly, underestimating him as many people did, and Henry snatched his arm away.

"I can walk, thank you," Henry seethed. Having recovered his arms, he straightened his suit jacket and put on a smile. *I'm not in the wrong here*, he thought. *The estate should have been mine from the start.*

"After you, sir," Sven said.

Henry looked over his shoulder as he left the ballroom to see Brooke and her mother yelling at each other, and he smiled—gratified at the riff he had caused. At least that had worked. It was good, but not enough—not nearly enough.

One way or another I will get a painting tonight, Henry vowed to himself as he was briskly led down the staircase. He just had to think, and outsmart these women.

How hard could it be?

32 REMARKS

Kathy stepped up the four steps to the stage and fumbled a bit as she took the microphone into her hands, remembering how Henry had been right there just a moment ago. She hoped that all was going to plan and that Henry would be arrested, with no one the wiser. Still, she had asked the modern quartet to continue playing during her remarks, only just reduced to mezzo violin.

She had spent the last month working on her remarks with rounds of feedback from Brooke. Her speech was intended to thank everyone who had come and those who had worked so diligently on the house, plus rally support for the collective, and encourage bookings at the hotel.

The crowd was sufficiently lubricated and appeared dazzled by her speech. In her closing remarks, Kathy encouraged people to make their way down to the gallery and let them know the doors would close tonight at nine.

Feeling optimistic and supremely curious as to how things resolved with Henry, she exited the stage to applause, shook some hands, and made her way down to the lobby.

33 CONFRONTATION

I *knew my mother was losing it, but good god*, Brooke thought as she coaxed Alice out of the ballroom and down to the lobby, determined to get her away from the guests gathered in the ballroom. Once near the restaurant, she spun around to face her mother. Furious with questions, she couldn't believe she was asking.

"How long? How long have you been dating Henry and hiding it from me?" asked Brooke, visibly angry.

"I told you I was here with him. Besides, what does it matter, honey? He's a very nice man."

Most people would be fooled by her innocent reply, but Brooke wasn't.

"He is *not* a nice man! Don't you remember me telling you all about the contest? About the murder? His father?" she said, stating what should have been incredibly obvious.

"I know what I was doing, Brooke. I was having a bit of fun, and besides, he flew me here to visit you—for over a month! That was my real motive."

"Your real motive? You were spying on me! Surely telling him all about what we were planning and working on, while Kathy and I were just sitting here, completely unaware. He is *dangerous*, Mother! I would have tightened the security had I known. You put us all in danger!" said Brooke, not holding back. "Not to mention Eddie! You just left him with the neighbors to come here and be with Henry? He hopes to get all C's! Do you even care that he won't be able to get into college with those grades? Are you even paying attention to your own kid?!"

Brooke paused, gathering herself. Her mother stood there quietly with her chin up.

Brooke continued in an eerily calm voice, "He just lost his dad, and you left him. What kind of mother are you?" she said in earnest disbelief.

"Oh, stop it, Brooke. You're making this into a big deal when it isn't one. So, I'm having a bit of fun. No one is getting hurt. Lighten up, would you?"

Brooke was reeling in disbelief – her mom was putting all their hard work in jeopardy. Despite everything, she still couldn't believe this was her mom. Her mother's behavior—deflecting the blame, refusing to take responsibility, and gaslighting when her daughter tried to hold her accountable.

Brooke felt helpless, and a tear began to run down her cheek when suddenly, a warm hand embraced hers. She looked up to find Travis.

"Brooke, I'm glad you're here. Your mother stopped by earlier and asked about us. I was trying to explain why I like you…you know, get her blessing," Travis said cautiously while analyzing both women, attempting to understand what he was walking into.

It occurred to Brooke then that her feelings weren't some fleeting thing. She wanted Travis, maybe even forever. Maybe she even wanted kids with him. Most of all, she wanted her mother to get lost.

"Hi, handsome," she said, looking at him as a momentary reprieve.

"Is everything okay here?" he asked.

"No, not really," Brooke replied truthfully, then relayed what had happened. "It's Henry. He was caught trying to blackmail us. Sven escorted him out. And my mother is his girlfriend." Anger began growing in Brooke's chest as she continued, "She deceived us all."

"Oh…" Travis responded, not knowing how to react to such an outrageous turn of events.

"Ah, everyone is here. Great," said Kathy tersely as she joined the group, then spoke to Brooke directly, "I've made the prepared announcements and all is on track upstairs. Brooke, what do you want to do now?" her business partner asked her.

Brooke knew Kathy was talking about her mother. What *did* she want to do? As she considered her options, she felt two squeezes on her hand and remembered Travis. He was there, holding her hand, calming her nerves. *I can do hard things*, she reminded herself.

"Mom, it's time for you to leave—do *not* come back. Not today, not tomorrow, never. I can't trust you, and I have enough to worry about."

Alice scoffed, "Well, you can't be serious? I'm your *mother*!"

"I'm absolutely serious," affirmed Brooke.

Alice mumbled something about her being a spoiled brat and threw her hands up in the air dramatically.

Kathy took that as her cue. "Here, I can help you leave," she said sternly to Alice.

"You'd like that, wouldn't you?" the jealous woman replied, showing her true colors as she moved toward the door. "I'll see myself out!" she said as she left in a hurry.

"I can't believe I just did that," Brooke admitted to Kathy once her mother was gone.

"I can. It was a long time coming from everything you told me."

Brooke nodded in agreement.

Now," Kathy said as she motioned to the English Basement, "we need to do something important."

34 LOVE

Hidden behind a bush across the street, Henry squinted at the glare on the large picture window in the front of the estate, trying desperately to see if Brooke, Travis, and Kathy had left the lobby. Alice had practically run out over twenty minutes ago, and he'd considered going back in then, but thought it best to wait and make sure Sven wasn't around.

The sun was starting to set, and he was looking more suspicious by the moment, so he decided it was now or never. He had a plan. A new plan. A very good plan.

He stepped out and casually walked to the crosswalk a half block away, and crossed back toward the estate. Instead of turning left to the doors, he carried on straight along the side of the Beaux-Arts exterior, ducking when reaching a window. Finally, he reached the end, where a weed-infested two-foot gap separated the mansion from the next building over—a department store, which was twice as tall. He approached the gap, inserted himself, and shimmied forward as far as he could amongst the long forgotten jungle of weeds. It had been a while since he saw this space and now estimated the halfway distance down the estate. Then he braced one foot on each building and placed his hands up and out, as if he was mid-jumping-jack, and climbed upward, moving one hand and foot at a time. His calves and biceps were killing him, but he persisted.

Just a little bit farther…there!

The façade of the estate ended suddenly about ten feet up,

revealing a tiny courtyard. Henry perched on the top, inspecting the best place to land. In the past, Oliver had neglected the courtyard, but these days, it was abundant with fresh vegetables and herbs. Henry released himself and, with a thump, fell into the garden and crouched amongst the tomato plants. The same old wooden door he remembered remained, but now, countless renovations later, he had no idea what to expect beyond it. He slowly crept forward and opened it.

He winced as the wood creaked loudly on the slightly rusted hinges and light poured down into the hall. Seeing no one, he slipped in and shut the door quickly, careful to make as little sound as possible. With a sigh of relief, he backed into the dark hallway that led to the old servants' staircase. Taking a moment to catch his breath, he let his eyes adjust to the dim interior. There was a new room down the hall about five paces on the right—well, not new exactly but renovated somehow. The door was slightly ajar, and he could see that several people were muttering and pointing inside it. Having no desire to get caught, he steeled himself and began to tip-toe up the old hidden staircase.

Once he reached the next floor, everything changed. The stairs became new, fully renovated, with brightly lit and painted walls, but the spacing remained—the stairwell was narrow and doubled back on itself every few paces. He stopped at each corner to make sure the coast was clear before moving forward. Reaching his destination at the top of the service stairs, he found a new door blocking the way. He slowly cracked it open. Seeing no one, he exited the stairwell and discovered the area that had once been the terrace and attic had been completely transformed. There was a glass-encased bathhouse on one side of the main stairs, and a strange old door with a peephole on the other. He had seen that door before. The speakeasy had been a hit during the dry run, and there were several pictures of the door on social media.

Stepping forward, he pressed his ear to the rough wood, then wiggled his fingers in the metal peephole, attempting to slide it open to peer inside. Hearing a couple laughing from the landing outside the ballroom just one floor down, he feared getting caught and went for it. After what felt like an eternity of wiggling, he was finally able to open the door.

It was very dark, and he could see next to nothing. Only a small beam of light came through the odd prohibition-inspired window. He shut the door behind him and took a minute to orient himself, eventually finding the light switch.

Turning it on, he took in the room entirely. He was shocked to see that the paintings were gone. *No, they have to be here somewhere,* he thought. He had been so thorough. He had hired a private detective for almost a year now, dedicated only to this. Surely, he would have seen if they had removed truckloads of paintings. With all the workers that came, items only ever went in; nothing much more than trash bags or old carpet rolls came out. *They have to be here.*

Henry started the tedious task of looking for a storage space, knowing that he could get caught at any moment, which would mean all his planning would be for nothing.

He moved furniture, looked under the bar, closely examined the new walls, and then finally went to the end of the room to the wall-to-wall bookcases. *Is there a hidden room, then?* he wondered, scanning the shelves for inconsistencies. Pulling a few books, he noticed that they all seemed to be normal, classic works, most of them leather-bound. Hemmingway, Walter Scott, Sinclair Lewis. He flipped through a couple, looking for a key embedded in the pages. No such luck. Then he noticed it—a minimal gap between the bookcases on the right-hand section. He raced over and began pulling everything off the shelf, from top to bottom. About halfway down, he pulled out a hardcover copy of Little Women, revealing a small black latch in the wood behind it.

He flipped the latch and with a tug, he easily pulled the entire bookcase section toward him. *This is it!*

Still afraid of being discovered, Henry entered the pitch-black space beyond the door quickly, shutting the swinging bookcase behind him. He bumbled around in the dark to discover another door in front of him, and he pushed the metal hip-height bar, but the door didn't budge. He turned around quickly to head back out the way he came, but that door, too, was locked.

It was then he noticed it, a tiny red light blinking just above a smooth glass surface, no larger than the size of a pencil eraser. A camera was embedded in the door, and had a clear view of his face.

"Fuck!" he muttered to himself. "Fuck, fuck, fuck!"

35 JUSTICE

Brooke knocked on the slightly ajar door of the new security room. As she stepped in, with Kathy following closely behind, she discovered Melissa and Sven were crammed in the former closet, staring at one particular computer screen displaying live footage.

"Wow, is that him?" said Brooke, both shocked and excited.

"Yep!" exclaimed Melissa, "he's trapped, completely trapped."

"Thank goodness we went through the trouble of securing the art!" said Kathy, utterly relieved that nothing had been stolen.

"Oh my god, this is incredible! You can see him so clearly! What do we do now, Melissa?" Brooke asked.

"Well, I'm glad you're here—I want to talk through options."

Melissa shared that they could cancel the grand opening celebration early, but neither Brooke nor Kathy wanted to make a scene. Instead, they decided they would try to have Henry arrested without interrupting the guests who were up in the ballroom, or wandering the corridors looking at art.

Brooke and Kathy couldn't take their eyes off the screen, gleefully watching Henry go ballistic as Melissa called the non-emergency police line and informed them of the situation.

About a half-hour later, two undercover officers arrived. Kathy went to the ballroom to continue to socialize with the guests, and Brooke escorted the officers to the security room, where they requested copies of the footage. They then made their way up the servants' staircase, through the speakeasy, and to the pull bookcase which was easy to identify since its contents had been clumsily scattered all over the floor.

Brooke stepped back to watch as the officers approached the bookcase door. She was scared but also thrilled, adrenaline making her shake. She had waited so long in fear, constantly questioning what Henry might do or when he might show up. Now that he was here and trapped, it was as if her body distrusted what her eyes were seeing. Everything was coming to a head. With bated breath, she watched the officers as if in slow motion.

She could hear her heart pounding in her ears as the officers counted down.

Three…

The taller officer readied himself to pull the shelf while the other drew his gun.

Two…

The officers looked at each other and nodded. They were ready.

One!

The tall officer pulled the latch. It clicked, and he pulled the door open toward Brooke so quickly that Henry, who had been leaning against the door, rolled backward. After he flopped onto the floor of the speakeasy, he opened his eyes and was immediately surprised to find a gun in his face.

Brooke stood frozen and watched as Henry scrambled toward the edge of the room. He then raised his hands in submission.

The officers made quick work of helping him to his feet while reading him his Miranda rights. Brooke stepped back toward the window while they passed her, Henry's eyes burning holes into her.

His fury was terrifying, and Brooke kept her distance as they made their way down the stairs. Midway down, Henry spotted a guest, and Brooke's worst fear was realized when he began shouting, "How dare you! These women have no right to this estate! It belongs to me! They are in league with a murderer! You hear that? A murderer!" he yelled at the officers, now struggling to keep his bucking body on his feet while continuing down the staircase.

Now unleashed, Brooke watched in horror as the wrathful man directed his ire at a guest. It was none other than a writer from the *New York Post* that Brooke had invited in her public relations effort.

"And Kathy—she's a fraud. A phony. A fake. She's selling cheap knockoffs for full price! See that painting? You're getting duped, man. Walk away!"

The journalist looked dismayed, raised an eyebrow at Brooke, and retreated away from the painting and the deranged guest being arrested.

The police officers made eye contact with the man briefly. Just then, still an entire floor above the lobby level, Henry used the distraction to elbow one officer, pull the gun from the holster of the other, and bolt forward, throwing the other officer off balance.

As the officer tripped down the stairs, Henry made a break for it, heading quickly toward Kathy, who stood paralyzed in the lobby, watching in horror.

Reaching the flat surface of the lobby, Henry righted himself and raised his right arm, holding the gun. Just then, a steel-toe-clad boot rose from behind him, and the officer kicked Henry's left calf hard from the staircase above. A sickening crack filled the air, and propelled him forward.

Henry landed face-first with a grunt. The gun was knocked free of his hand and slid easily on the freshly buffed flooring and the officers moved in quickly with handcuffs.

And as suddenly as it had started, it was over.

They had him now.

Brooke slipped behind the officers over to Kathy, and clung to her partner in an all-encompassing hug. Happy tears came rapidly as they watched the officers work. Once Henry was securely in the back of the cop car, Brooke flipped him the bird through the window and headed up to her office to call Andrew, their lawyer.

Approaching the office door, Brooke stopped abruptly. The writer from the *Post* was there on his phone. She heard him let the other person on the line know he would call them back just as she reached the door handle. He looked at her, expectant.

She thought of all she wanted to say—*I'm so sorry, that was a former contestant, and he was deranged, you're safe now*—but she didn't want the follow-up questions the reporter would inevitably ask.

"Can I help you?" was the only thing she could think of that kept her neutral—not giving anything to the press, at least for now.

"Well, your event was lovely up until just then. I'm hoping I might interview you to understand what exactly just happened on the stairs," the man said politely.

"Oh. Of course. Not today, though. I can't think straight..." she admitted with a deep exhale. She needed to talk to Kathy and get their story straight. Waving her hand toward the stairs, she added, "For obvious reasons. You must be tired, too. Tomorrow? I'll make myself available."

"Yes, that works," the journalist replied, "I'll give you a call in the morning."

Brooke nodded back and opened her office door.

He got what he wanted, she thought in disbelief. *Henry made a scene on purpose—he can ruin us still.*

Brooke's conversation with Andrew was brief but reassuring. Apparently, between the security camera footage and Henry's behavior toward the officers, they had a strong case against him. The moment Andrew hung up, Brooke melted onto her bed, fully clothed and utterly relieved. She hadn't realized how much stress she was holding in her body, simply because Henry was at large.

After a few moments of utter bliss, her thoughts turned to the *Post* interview and her responsibilities. She lay there trying to sort out what to say, until an unexpected text message arrived.

36 TOAST

What a day it had been. Kathy was completely exhausted. The grand opening had its ups and downs, and now there was only one important thing left to do.

Tonight was the last night that the estate would truly be theirs alone, since hotel operations went into full swing the following day. With that in mind, Kathy wanted to have a small, private celebration. Not a long, drawn-out thing, but she had planned something special for Brooke.

She assumed her partner was roaming around the estate, so she texted her to meet her in the parlor room in half an hour.

Kathy was ready when Brooke arrived, looking as exhausted as she felt. She sat in one of the leather chairs closest to the fireplace, and positioned the white box with a simple red ribbon on her lap. She wondered if it was enough, considering all that Brooke had done for her, for them. Brooke was the best business partner she could imagine—even with the news of her daughter and the wedding, Brooke took everything in her stride. Kathy couldn't help but feel loved. Truly. Who knew you could feel a kind of sisterly love with a business partner?

Travis was ready, too. Kathy had come to him a few days ago and told him her plan. Wanting to help make tonight special, he had set out a decadent charcuterie spread and poured three glasses of Eleanor's champagne that she'd gifted the pair.

Tabitha was there too, on the loveseat nearest the curtains, watching from a safe distance where she would not be bothered.

Brooke entered the room, and Kathy stood, holding the box.

"Oh, you shouldn't have!" Brooke said with faux coyness to both Kathy and Travis, as he handed her a glass of champagne and kissed her forehead.

"Brooke," Kathy began, "I am so incredibly proud of you, and proud of us. That afternoon you came to me and dragged me up to the attic, I had no idea what you were capable of. I suspected you were brilliant and determined, but I just…I had no idea." She paused and fought her emotions—she had vowed to herself not to cry.

"And," she continued with determination, "your positivity and calm confidence inspires me to not hold back. To just go for it. I think we have something here. I think we'll be a wild success, and it's all because of you. I'm incredibly proud to call you my partner. Cheers, Brooke!"

She raised her glass, and Travis said, "Hear, hear!"

Their glasses clinked, and they all took a sip, savoring the champagne and their collective success.

Then Kathy continued, "And there's someone else I know who is cheering you on from afar. I thought we could bring her a bit closer to us every day with this…"

Kathy handed Brooke her gift, and watched closely as she untied the bow, and gingerly opened the package. Then, realizing what it was, the trio began laughing uncontrollably.

Travis, knowing what it was supposed to be but never having seen the infamous Polaroid, went to Brooke's side to take a peek. When he realized it was the photograph of Eleanor topless on a beach, he gasped and quickly looked away, blushing furiously. The infamous Polaroid that Eleanor had sent them had been blown up onto a square canvas and framed.

After the laughter had died down, Kathy hugged Brooke and then made her way to the door.

"Wait, you're leaving?" Brooke asked.

"Yes, I was thinking about it. Is there something else?" Kathy asked.

Brooke told her about the journalist, and the women quickly made a plan. Kathy had talked to the press plenty during her career and was confident about what should be shared. Travis engaged in the conversation thoughtfully, occasionally suggesting that the reporter may ask this question or that. Within a short amount of time, Brooke felt confidently armed with all potential talking points recorded on her phone.

At a natural moment, Kathy made her exit.

"Brooke, I'm heading to bed, but I think Travis would like to thank you, too." She gave him a wink and closed the door behind her.

Kathy was utterly exhausted, but also the happiest she had been in years.

37 GUESTS

The next morning, Brooke made her way downstairs to find everything in order. The hotel and restaurant staff were diligently getting prepped for their first full day's service. Before long, Kathy joined her on the sofa in the lobby to wait for Andrew.

"So, how did last night go?" asked Kathy, suspecting everything Brooke could definitely not bring herself to tell her.

"Very well," she said coyly.

"Oh?" Kathy replied, politely pressing for details.

"Well, we talked for a bit, and then…we didn't really talk the rest of the night." She giggled. "We were *too busy*," she said, with intentional inuendo.

"Ladies! Good to see you!" interrupted Andrew, just as Kathy opened her mouth to respond. Their outstanding lawyer had excellent timing, though Brooke was unsure how much detail she wanted to provide to her business partner.

Andrew's update was thorough and thoroughly enjoyable. Henry was in a holding cell and had been questioned. At first, he denied his intentions, but then his lawyer, Chip—who was, by chance, Andrew's college buddy—advised him to tell the truth. Technically, he did not steal a painting, only attempted it, but he *did* assault an officer, violate his agreement, and was trespassing. Although minor offenses, Andrew assured the pair that they added up and were now on his permanent record. He suggested the women file a formal restraining order against him and, with their consent, Andrew agreed he would have his team do all the paperwork. Brooke was relieved to hear that Henry would not bother them again.

Shortly after Andrew left, the wedding planner, Juliet, arrived. Now that the grand opening had passed, Brooke wanted to get started right away—there were only a few short weeks until the main event. She picked up her laptop and started the video meeting so that Elizabeth could be included, too.

Brooke outlined what she and Elizabeth had discussed—a family-only reception in the speakeasy the evening before, the atrium and terrace transformed into a lush location for the wedding ceremony itself, and a large seated dinner and dancing in the ballroom. She proceeded to share the collaborations they had secured—*Architectural Digest* had agreed to do a photo-heavy spread, anticipating the estate would look incredible, while a local florist had agreed to provide the flowers at wholesale, and do the arrangements. Plus, Travis had convinced a local French bakery to make the cake and prepare petit fours for dessert.

"But why," Juliet asked, "don't you have the budget to outsource everything? Surely, it would help expedite the process—and I have the connections. I could arrange everything."

"True, but the reason I did this was because *AD* has agreed to promote our wedding venue. Their audience is the most important part of the collab," Brooke explained, adding that they needed the wedding planner to know and take care of all the odds and ends.

Then, all of a sudden, two very unexpected guests came through the door, luggage in hand.

"Is that who I think it is?" asked Kathy.

"Well, who else would it be? No one else would dare stroll into the best new hotel in the city without reservations!" replied Eleanor in all her sassy glory.

Brooke set the laptop down on the coffee table and rushed to Eleanor, embracing her in a big hug.

Kathy stood and shook Oliver's hand as the foursome all greeted each other warmly—the wedding planner and Elizabeth now wholly forgotten.

"I'm shocked. How are you here? Why are you here? Do you need a room? I would offer you your room, but it's been completely transformed, and your things have been relocated," said Brook in a flurry.

"Oh no," Elcanor Beaufort said, waving her hand dismissively, "that won't be necessary. We're on a long layover on our way to Telluride, so I thought I'd pop in and see everything myself." She removed her oversized black designer sunglasses. "The website and pictures online are splendid…but I have to say, the real thing is even better! Brooke, you've truly outdone yourself."

"Thank you! I've been working my ass off for the last year. Your approval means a lot," said Brooke, beaming.

"Oh dear, don't work yourself up into a lather. Now, where's Travis? Oliver would like to talk to him—you know, give him some pointers to make sure he keeps you happy," she said with a mischievous smirk.

"What! Not you, too? Has Travis told absolutely everyone? I think I'm going to die of embarrassment…" replied Brooke, holding the cold backs of her hands to her flushed cheeks.

"Not me, specifically, but you must know that Travis and Oliver are constantly messaging. Any time we get Wi-Fi, his phone goes wild, dinging like crazy. Don't be embarrassed, dear—he's quite a catch. And well, it seems you are taking after me a bit," she said with sultry pride.

Brooke then solicited Eleanor's advice on how to keep both their romantic and professional relationship intact.

"It wasn't an easy thing at first," Eleanor explained, "but then after a while, it comes naturally, and it's wonderful to have someone who understands the whole of what you are going through. Lucky girl you are, you have that with two people—Kathy and Travis."

After more convincing, Brooke admitted to herself that it did sound like a beautiful life. They soon headed into the new dining room to catch up and test Travis's dinner menu together.

38 ART

The next morning, Kathy checked her phone first thing in bed, as she often did. Today, she received an unusual message from Brooke. A buyer had contacted her and completed the sale of the Bansky painting with the finance chair of the board, and they were requesting Kathy hand-deliver it this morning—in the next hour.

Kathy sat up straight in bed, shaking off sleep and rereading the message to make sure she wasn't dreaming.

Not wanting to waste time arguing over text, Kathy verified the deposit in the art collective account, carefully packaged the painting, and set out to the address. Melissa drove and then escorted her upstairs to the penthouse suite of a very luxurious tower of condos overlooking Central Park.

Kathy had never done this sort of thing—she had always had art preparers and art handlers. As she exited the elevator holding the wrapped Banksy, she was terrified she had irreparably ruined what this mysterious collector had just paid a small fortune for. She knocked on the door quickly while holding the painting directly in front of her so the edges didn't catch anything. Melissa waited two paces behind her, politely ignoring her struggle.

"Ah, that must be my painting," said a masculine voice as he came to the door.

Kathy thought the man sounded familiar. She snapped her head to the side of the painting, and then saw none other than Ronan Sebastian Aetos, shirtless and grinning ear to ear.

"Ummm, oh…" mumbled Kathy.

"It's not often I render a woman speechless. Brooke mustn't

have told you," he snickered. "Come in, come in." He gently brushed her hands as he took the canvas from her.

I'm going to kill Brooke! thought Kathy, as she instructed Melissa to head back to the estate, then walked into the small yet immaculate suite.

As Sebastian carried the parcel away, Kathy was drawn to the panorama view of the city. She stared for a moment and told herself to relax, but still couldn't shake the sensation that this was somehow about more than a painting. She could feel Sebastian's presence, even from the other room. Something had happened in the atrium, and likely in the gallery, something electrifying—she thought maybe there was a chance he felt the same. Gathering her courage, she then turned back to the handsome man re-entering the room.

"Sebastian, thank you very much for your purchase. Your generosity will do wonders to help the art collective thrive. But…" She paused a moment, unsure how to say what she meant without offending him. "May I ask, why did you buy it? You've been so generous, but you were so reluctant when we first met in your office…I'm just trying to make sense of things."

"Ha!" he replied abruptly.

Was everything a game to him? thought Kathy, somewhat irritated.

Then he moved toward her, and she inched backward, her back touching the floor-to-ceiling glass window. He continued forward until there wasn't an inch between them. Kathy looked upward, trying to understand this cryptic man, while he looked down at her with a smirk on his face. She could feel his rapid breaths on her, see his chiseled pecs next to her chin, and feel the heat radiating from his body.

She yearned to touch every inch of him.

Finally, he spoke. "You are one of the most fascinating women I've ever met. You're beautiful yet humble, not to mention incredibly intelligent. I want you." He reached his hand up between them and nudged her chin upward, gently aligning their lips, and whispered a solitary request.

"Kiss me?"

Kathy studied him carefully, seeing the kindness in him—not for the first time, but fully now—and responded. She kissed him and let herself go. Who knows how long they just kissed, exploring each other, holding each other near the window.

At some point, Kathy found herself nibbling and kissing his

collarbone, shoulders, and neck. He removed her suit jacket and then her blouse and knelt before her, kissing her breasts and stomach, revering her body—even the softer wrinkled parts.

If seduction is an art, then Sebastian is Michelangelo, she decided. He took his time, and moved with slow care and adoration. In short, it made her want to rip his pants off. She was lost to him for a while, before she came to her senses.

"Wait, wait!" she said, trying to get a grip. He paused, stood, faced her, and held her hands, waiting for her, unhurried. "I…I don't do one-time things. Is that what you want? Is that why you asked me here?" she asked earnestly.

"Sorry, I'm doing this all wrong. It's just that you looked so beautiful standing in my place, and I couldn't help myself. I…look, I really like you, and I want us to date. No, not date. I want to be in a relationship. Are you seeing anyone?" He stepped back and rubbed his face. "God, of course you are." He shook his head at himself, annoyed.

How does he see me? Kathy wondered while watching this man, who could likely have any gorgeous woman he wanted, struggle to express his feelings.

She considered his request. She wanted it all and decided then and there that she would never settle for less. Stepping forward, she put her hand on his chest to stop him from spiraling and said, "No, I'm not seeing anyone, and I really like you too. I'd like to have a relationship with you, and I don't play around. I want something serious. I don't know if you have kids, but have one. She's grown and out of the house, so I'm done having them. I want someone I can grow old with, and if you think that might be you, let's try it."

As Kathy laid out exactly what she wanted, she watched Sebastian's eyes light up. It was the best thing she had seen in a long time, and lately, she had seen many good things.

Kathy wanted Sebastian and that morning, she made sure she got exactly what she wanted.

39 PARTNERS

Water splashed out onto the atrium floor as Brooke enthusiastically cheered on Kathy in the next claw-foot tub over. The sun had set, and there were only two guests in the hotel, so the partners had decided to continue their wind-down routine—only now with swimsuits.

So much had happened, and they had a lot to discuss.

"I knew it! When he called me to ask how to buy that painting, I just knew it. Then the personal delivery request confirmed my suspicions," Kathy laughed in reply, clearly delighted.

"I want a play-by-play!" Brooke demanded.

Kathy modestly explained what had happened. How she was shocked when Sebastian answered the penthouse door, and later how she laid out exactly what she wanted.

Brooke was remarkably proud of her partner and wondered, *why don't I do that more often?* She then vowed to herself that she would.

Itching to move out of the spotlight, Kathy changed the subject.

"Now that you and Travis are an item, how is it going?"

After Brooke had made their relationship official, Kathy hadn't heard much. Sure, she had seen them giving each other fond glances and laughing easily together the way new couples do, but she needed to know more. She needed to know if their relationship was on track, and if the head of their restaurant business was happy.

"Well, after Eleanor's comment about Travis and Oliver

texting, I demanded to see his phone," Brooke shared with a satisfied smirk.

"You did not!" Kathy said, eyes bulging in proud disbelief.

"And? Find any juicy gossip?"

"Yes and no. There was quite a bit of talk about recipes and plating, but…there were a few key texts about us."

"Us as in you and me, or us as in you and Travis?"

"Both!" Brooke clarified.

"Do tell!" Kathy demanded.

Brooke shared that Travis had been asking Oliver for advice about how best to work with them both, and he had given sound and somewhat generic advice a while back after they had first won the contest.

"Travis told Oliver about the fits and starts of our relationship. It was helpful to read his perspective—I think he was really struggling with what was the right thing to do, even though he liked me. I'd been questioning whether he liked me at all, and it turned out he did the whole time. More recently, he asked Oliver how to keep a strong-willed woman happy!" Brooke shared with a chuckle.

"Oliver would know! Such a good question," remarked Kathy, ready to take his sage advice as she looked over at Brooke submerged in the tub, eyes closed, with a serene grin on her face.

"And?" she prompted.

"Oh! Well, it was a simple response. 'Anytime you are confused, simply ask her what she wants, and then believe what she says.' "

"So simple."

"Yes, simple but effective. I've caught Travis asking it several times now, and I love it. I tell him exactly what I want, and there's no second-guessing, no questioning. It's amazing."

The partners laughed and then stilled in gratitude for several comfortable minutes, enjoying their hot soak and the subtle breeze coming through the terrace entrance.

Kathy was the first to break the silence. "Thank you, Brooke," she said simply.

"For what?" Brooke replied.

"For everything," Kathy explained. "I'm in awe of you. The renovations you did to the hotel—handling all those details—the results are just incredible. The restaurant, the dry run, the marketing—not to mention the grand opening; I mean, you had it all planned in fifteen-minute increments! And despite everything that happened with Henry, and your mother…"

Brooke looked to her partner, whose head was visible above the tub, as Kathy continued, "And…and when the malicious email appeared, and my integrity was called into question—you trusted me. That's a big deal, Brooke. That alone could have been enough for you to suggest I resign, but you didn't." Kathy shook her head in humble disbelief, looking down at the still water.

"And *then* my daughter demanding a wedding here on top of everything else on your plate. And there I was, being an absolute jerk and telling Travis not to date you while you encouraged my relationship with Sebastian behind the scenes—you handled it all with such grace."

Kathy looked up to find Brooke staring at her intently, tears of joy running down her face.

"I didn't feel graceful," Brooke admitted earnestly.

"You were. Thank you," Kathy stated confidently.

Brooke smiled at Kathy and then closed her eyes. She couldn't help but think of how lucky she was. After the grand opening fiasco, the journalist published the story of Henry's attempted art theft, and the publicity had been incredibly good for business. The hotel was booked at eighty percent capacity for nearly a year, the restaurant was bustling at every service, there were event requests coming in daily, and she and Travis were in love. Meanwhile, Kathy had private buyers contacting her for viewings, and she was enjoying her new romance with Sebastian.

And the glue holding everything together? Their audacious partnership.

Together, women are unstoppable.

40 INVITATION

Eleanor had her hiking boots securely fastened as she made her way on the hemlock bark trail, past a thick grove of green cedar trees. Oliver had scouted the spot a few days after they arrived in Telluride.

As the sprightly woman exited the cool, dark underbrush of the forest just a half mile from their chalet, she entered a clearing surrounded by purple flowers with green leaves jutting out of the earth, reaching knee height. Oliver, the love of her life, was there in the clearing, a blanket already laid out, and he was arranging items just so from a picnic basket.

Eleanor joined him and set herself down gingerly, laying a hand on her man, still handsome in his late seventies. They sat silently side by side, looking to where a boulder dropped dramatically to a ravine, revealing a stunning meadow with a river winding through it.

It was a serene moment. Or it was until modern-day technology interrupted it—a rare text message chimed in Eleanor's pocket.

"It could be an emergency. Let me check it quickly," she said to Oliver.

Brooke: Dear Eleanor, I don't know your mailing address, so I thought I'd text you.

Eleanor: Fair. And?

Brooke: I'm writing to formally invite you to a wedding at the estate. Kathy's daughter Elizabeth is getting married, and we're hosting the ceremony and reception here. It will be over the-top as it's a bit of a marketing stunt, and we would love it if you and Oliver could attend!

"Oh my, Oliver! You'll never guess what…"

"What is it, lovely? Don't leave me in suspense—I want to get back to the quiet," he replied dryly.

She read him the text.

"Well, we have to go!" she added with genuine enthusiasm. "The only other wedding we hosted was secret in the eighties, with only three people and a justice of the peace. I cannot *wait* to see the grand décor Brooke comes up with!"

Oliver gave a simple affirmative nod in agreement.

Eleanor: We will be there with bells on! Please email me the details. Xoxo.

The End

ABOUT THE AUTHOR

A storyteller who loves to dwell in the gray areas of the human experience, Corinne Cavanaugh enjoys unpacking politically and emotionally charged topics. Her writing serves up fun, unapologetic opinions and an opportunity to identify with another person's experience in a non-confrontational way. She writes a blog and contemporary fiction novels for book club readers.

Corinne holds a Master's Degree in International Relations from Harvard University, has had a career in marketing and serves on boards.

She resides in the Seattle area and spends her free time reading books, petting cats, and keeping her toddlers alive.

THANK YOU

Thank you so very much for taking the time to read the second novel in the Audacious Series. I would be ever so grateful if you could please leave a public review on the Amazon or Goodreads listing.

The last book in the series, *An Audacious Love*, is available on Amazon! Enter into Eleanor and Oliver's adventures and love story as they visit historically significant destinations all over the globe, and return to the hotel for Elizabeth's wedding!

Please follow me online to keep in touch! I am on: Instagram, Facebook, TikTok and X. Learn more at AudaciousBook.com.

#BeAudacious

Xoxo,
Corinne

Made in the USA
Columbia, SC
25 November 2024

47064285R00087